Home on the Trail

by Mona Exinger

A Fireside Library Book

OGDEN PUBLICATIONS INC.
Topeka, Kansas

Copyright © 1999 by Mona Exinger
All rights reserved.
No part of this book may be used or reproduced
in any manner whatsoever without written permission
except in the case of brief quotations
embodied in critical articles and reviews.

Published by Ogden Publications
1503 S.W. 42nd St., Topeka, Kansas 66609

Publisher: Bryan Welch
Editor-in-Chief: Ann Crahan
Senior Editor: Jean Teller
Art Director: Diane Rader

For more information about
Ogden Publications titles,
or to place an order, please call:
(Toll-free) 1-800-678-4883

Cover from a painting by William Henry Jackson,
courtesy of Scotts Bluff National Monument,
Gering, Neb.
Western Emigrant Trails (1830-1870) maps
used with permission
of the Oregon-California Trails Association,
Independence, Mo.

ISBN 0-941678-63-6
Second printing, May 2000
Printed and bound in the United States of America

Fireside Library

Other books in the Fireside Library

These Lonesome Hills	Letha Boyer
Home in the Hills	Letha Boyer
Of These Contented Hills	Letha Boyer
The Talking Hills	Letha Boyer
Born Tall	Garnet Tien
The Turning Wheel	Garnet Tien
The Farm	LaNelle Dickinson Kearney
The Family	LaNelle Dickinson Kearney
Lizzy Ida's Luxury	Zoe Rexroad
Lizzy Ida's Tennessee Troubles	Zoe Rexroad
Lizzy Ida's Mail Order Grandma	Zoe Rexroad
Mandy to the Rescue	Zoe Rexroad
Carpenter's Cabin	Cleoral Lovell
Quest for the Shepherd's Son	Juanita Killough Urbach
Martin's Nest	Ellie Watson McMasters
Third Time for Charm	Mabel Killian
To Marry a Stranger	Glenda McRae
Pledges in the West	Glenda McRae
Sod Schoolhouse	Courtner King and Bonnie Bess Worline
Texas Wildflower	Debra Hall
River Run To Texas	George Chaffee
Aurora	Marie Kramer

Dedication

This book is for my father,
William Friedrichs,
for whom I first wrote this story.

– **Mona Exinger**

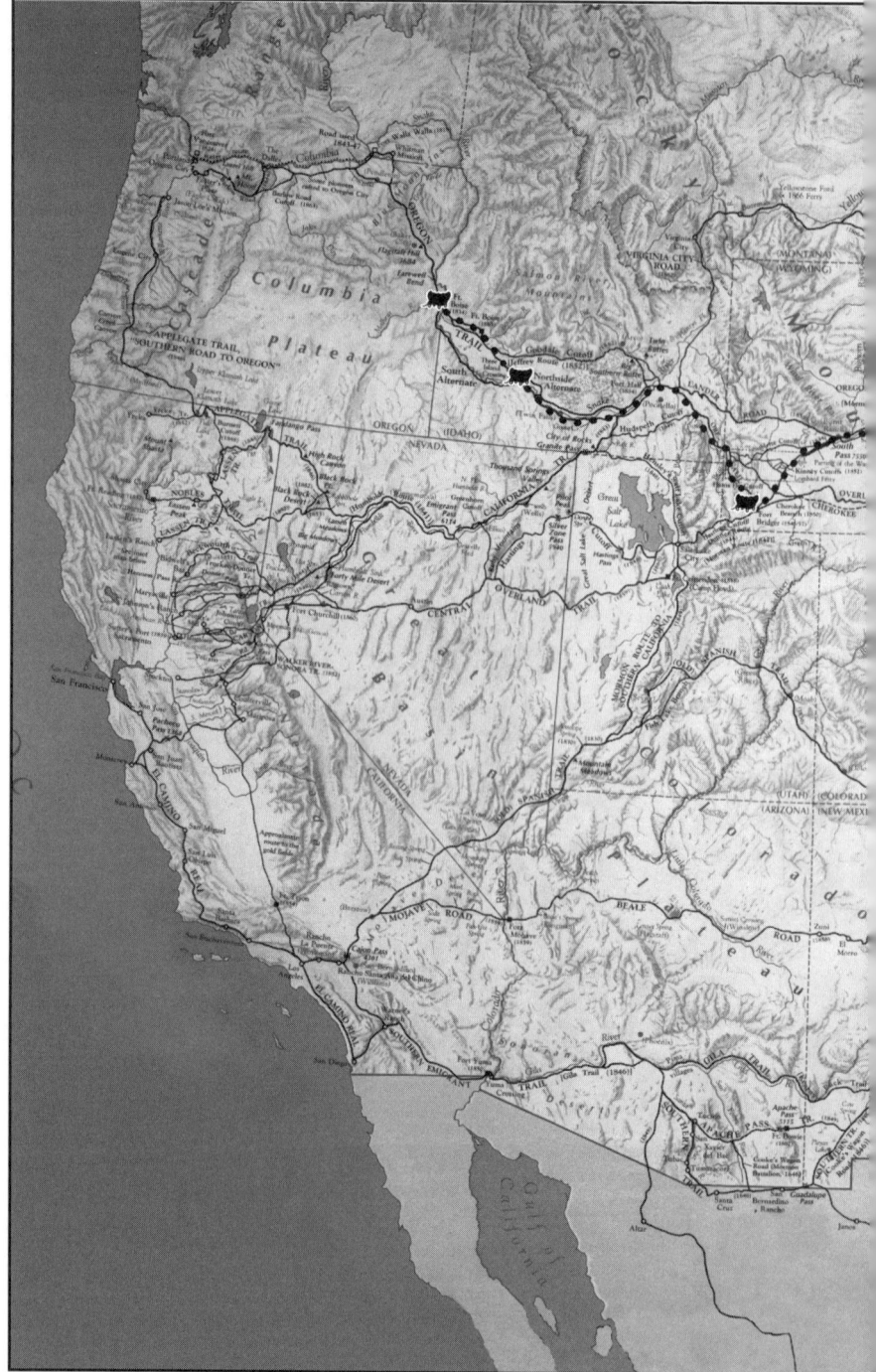

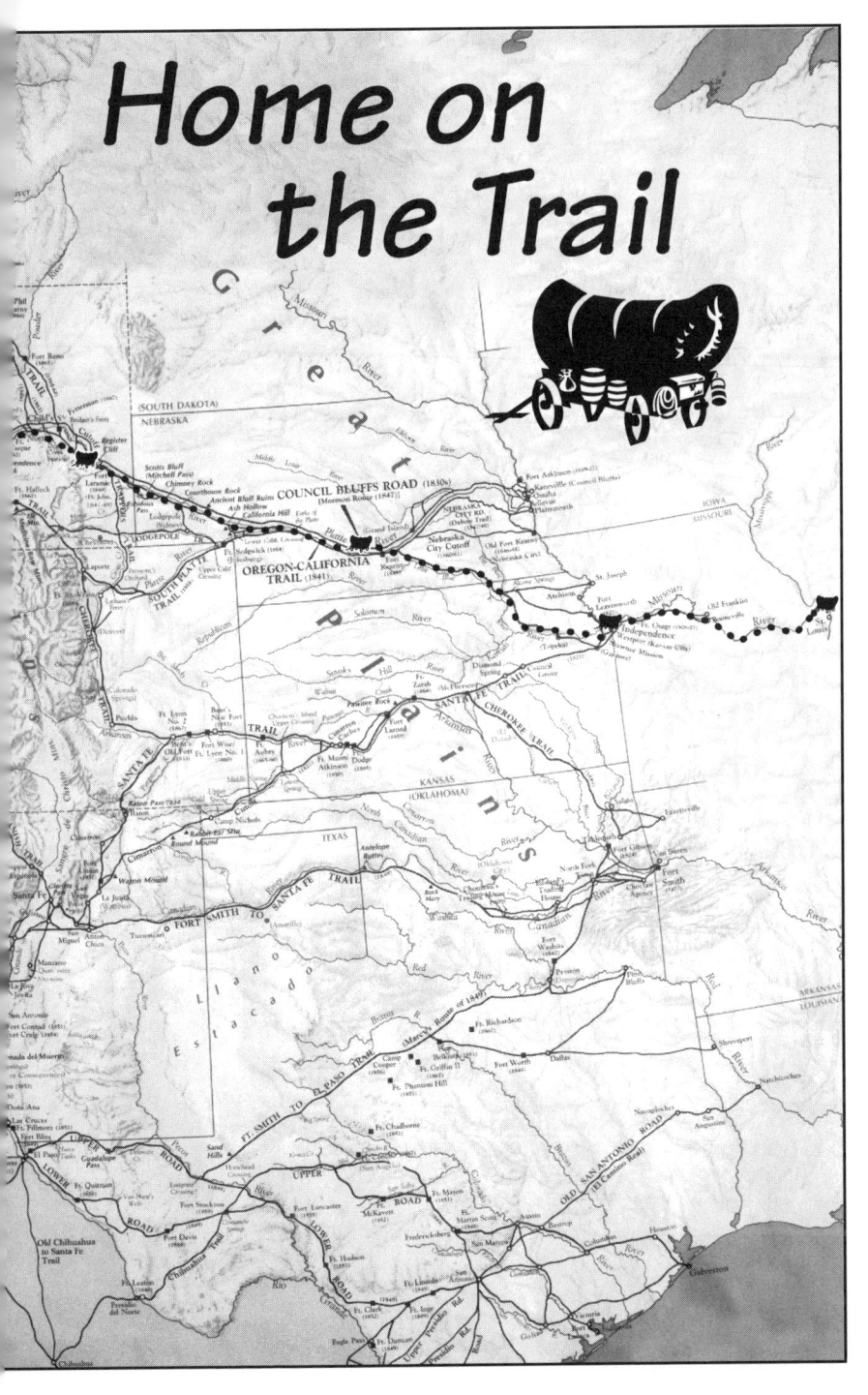

Chapter One

November

November 15 –

Things weren't ever the same for our family after the day Marcus met Cyrus Bates. We'd come to town, and I was over at the mercantile, keeping one eye on what I was getting for my egg money and the other on the children. Marcus was supposed to be getting the blue roan a new shoe for the one it threw two days ago. Well, he was at the blacksmith all right, but the conversation there was heating up faster than the smith's fire. The men were herded together to jaw about what we called Oregon fever, a popular sickness lately here in Michigan.

It wasn't until I'd finished with the store-

Home on the Trail

keeper that I realized Marcus had been gone long enough to get four shoes on the horse and a couple on himself. I was heading across the street, back to the wagon, telling Hester to keep hold of Matthew's hand, when here comes Marcus bustling up with the roan. He didn't look nearly as guilty as I figured he ought to for lollygagging about so long. He hitched the horse to the wagon, saying nothing but with a thoughtful look on his face. As for myself, I held my peace while we loaded up and most of the way home. Then curiosity got the better of me, and I allowed to Marcus as how he'd been quite awhile getting the horse shod. He just smiled and said yes, they'd got to talking some. He didn't say any more, and I didn't have time to ask, because Matt dropped his licorice whip on the floor of the wagon bed, and I had to lean back and search for it, then wipe off the dirt.

Later that evening, I'd just put the children to bed and settled down to work on the gray stockings I was knitting for Hester, when Marcus puts his book down and says what would I think about going to Oregon next spring?

Well, it wasn't as much of a surprise as you might imagine. This Oregon fever has been going on for some time, with people packing up and making the long trip to where there's better land and more of it. Marcus and I have had a touch of the fever ourselves – as we are not against trying something new every so often – and we'd already talked about it, thinking we might go in a couple more years.

But one look at that man's face, and I told myself it was going to be a couple years sooner than I'd bargained on. I could see his mind was made up. So I said I guessed maybe I could go to Oregon next spring, and by the way, was he going along, too, and should we take time to pack up the children while we were at it?

Then he laughed, and I laughed, and it looked like it was settled, so he told me about Cyrus Bates.

A few weeks back, Marcus had gotten wind this Bates fellow was trying to get some folks together for a wagon train out to Oregon. So when Mr. Bates happened along at the blacksmith's that afternoon to spread a little of his fever on the subject, the two of them had a chance for a good long talk – long enough for Marcus to make up his mind about both Mr. Bates and Oregon.

Cyrus Bates lived about thirty miles south of town. He was quite well-to-do, with his big farm in Michigan, but that didn't save him from the fever. He decided he could just as well be well-to-do in Oregon instead. Last

Home on the Trail

year, he took his oldest son, Rafe, and tagged along with a wagon train going out that way. After they got to Oregon, Mr. Bates found himself a fine piece of land and left Rafe there to get their farm started. Then he made his way back East this year, coming with a load of traders who supply some of the Army forts strung out along the trail.

Next spring, he's going to pack up Mrs. Bates and the rest of their family and move them all out, along with any others who'll go with them.

Marcus told me he could see Bates was a good man and would be a fine leader, something you have to be careful about, since the right leader makes all the difference in whether you even get to Oregon at all – or so we hear. And it sounded that way to me, too: Mr. Bates is the kind who decides he wants to do something, then plans it all out and does it right.

We'll have to pay some for him to guide us, and although he's not one of those mountain men who's been through the land a great deal, he did go through it every step of the way himself.

Marcus and I decided to trust what Mr. Bates has to say. As for the rest, we just hope for the best. My ma always says that, and it seems to fit here.

Mona Exinger

November 22 –

One day, the idea of keeping this diary jumped up and hitched itself onto my head. A trip to Oregon is a big thing in your life, and it might be important to have a record of it. Lots of interesting things are bound to happen, and I won't forget too many of them if I keep this with me and add to it from time to time. Who knows? Maybe someday, somebody'll read it over and find a use for it. Well, maybe.

I'd best tell about the family now. Our name is Edmondson. It's just me – my name's Martha – my husband, Marcus, and our children Hester and Matthew. We're not a large family by any respects, but plenty for me to keep track of, at home or on the trail.

Marcus is a big enough man, not tall, but something to put your arms around, and sturdy, which is the kind of man you want to have with you on a trip out West – or any other time. He has a cheery smile that peeks out of the middle of his bristly beard. He smiles pretty often, since he's good-natured and likes to tease me. Marcus was real smart in school and still reads a lot, which most grown men don't take the time for. He's handy, too, and always comes up with new ideas on things. Makes me feel the fool some-

Home on the Trail

times, but I'm handy myself in some ways around the house, and he loves me just the same.

Our girl Hester is a quiet child mostly and pretty serious for nine years old, although she gets feisty like me sometimes. She's sharp as a tack in school and reads a lot like her pa. Those big brown eyes take in whatever's around them. She gets sassy with her little brother sometimes and pretends she's got no use for him, but it's just an act. She'll turn up her nose and flip her braids at him one minute, then the next, sit down and help him untie a knot in his shoelaces. Hester's a sweet helper around the house, too, but I don't like to work my children hard the way some folks do. I believe she needs time to herself to play, besides her chores and schoolwork.

No need to worry about Matthew getting enough time for play – at six, he's a handful, there's no getting around it – and a challenge to keep clean. He'll race inside for a piece of bread and honey and smile through the dirt on his face, like Marcus does through his beard. I say trouble seems to know where to find him. Marcus says it isn't really trouble, but adventure, so I reckon Matt'll have more than the rest of us on the way to Oregon. My boy has a good heart, though, and doesn't really mean any badness. He's just little. I have to laugh and forgive him his sins, same as God does with all of us, I guess.

November 29 –

Marcus and I have farmed our land in Michigan for eleven years now, ever since we got married. We're hard workers and have made a good job of it: smooth, neat fields with nary a stump in sight, a snug little house, and our animals, fat and sleek, filling the barn. It's more than many can say, and we're proud of what we've done. It came as some surprise to our families when we broke the news about going to Oregon. They must have thought we'd stay and be buried here in the end, we had such a nice place going.

But the truth was bound to wiggle out somehow, and the way it came about was that Marcus went to my brother Robert and asked if he'd like to buy our farm. Robert was still helping my pa work the big old home place, but he'd been fidgety to get his own land so he could marry Eleanor Hoffstetter. He's been courting and pining after her for nearly two years.

Marcus figured it all out that Robert could get himself a fine farm and hitched to Eleanor in the bargain, and we'd wind up

Home on the Trail

with a nest egg for expenses to Oregon. I was glad of the plan, since I couldn't bear to leave our home to just anyone. But Eleanor's a smart girl, and orderly, and I expect she'll keep the place as nice as I would myself.

Lightning had nothing on how fast the news traveled once it was out. Friends and neighbors dropped in to say their various pieces on whether it was a wise thing or not, and I began to see how hard it would be to leave all the good people here.

The hardest part was when Mary Ann brought me the apple pie, which was sad and funny at the same time. Mary Ann is Marcus' younger sister and my best friend in all the world. Her pies always win blue ribbons at the county fair. Apple is my very favorite that she makes, and when she heard the news of us leaving, she baked me a great big one and hurried right over with it.

I was putting water on to boil for the wash when I happened to look out the window and see her stumbling into the yard, sobbing all over that pie she was so heartbroken. Poor Mary Ann! On account of her tears, she couldn't see where she was going and tripped over that pesky elm root that always seems to reach out and grab a body. I dropped the tub of water all over the floor on my way out the door, just as Mary Ann went down and the pie flew up in the air. The pie's wings lasted long enough to turn it neatly over so it could fall top-crust down in the dirt.

To make a long story short, I got Mary Ann in the house, mopped up the water, and set us both down to have a cup of tea and piece of pie. I'd done my best to pick up the pie and put it back together, and it was really the best I've ever had – and only a little gritty.

When we got together with Marcus' folks and mine for a big Sunday dinner to celebrate the news, they all let loose on what fools we were, turning our backs on such a lovely farm and years of hard work only to traipse off into the wilderness and do it all over again – if we weren't eaten by bears or Indians first. They made a yakkity ruckus all through dinner – even during the cake and pie and coffee. It was loud enough not only for us to hear, but also any of the neighbors who hadn't yet.

Of course, it was in the children's hearing, too, and my piece of applesauce cake kind of soured in my mouth when I saw poor Matthew slink off in the corner to share a few tears with the wall. Hester slipped after him, sat down close and patted his knee, looking more than a little worried that all the family should be so cross.

Now it's my opinion everyone ought to be

Home on the Trail

free to have their say, and goodness knows, I take the advice often enough myself. But seeing the children so upset was hard on me, especially after we'd tried to tell them the long trip to Oregon and a new life would be such a good thing. There's a short walk to the end of my temper, and the folks had hurried it along considerably. So I finally piped up that since it was the Lord's Day, we should all be thankful for having time together now, not harping on when we mightn't be, later. Everyone slowed down to a grumble, and the talk turned to other matters, so I said my Sunday prayer for that, and meant it.

Truth be told, I'd argued some in my own mind about Oregon.

We'd be leaving the only folks we'd known all our lives, never knowing when we might see any of them again. And it was clear as day some of these dear ones thought we were doing a foolish thing. Between a rock and a hard place, we were, putting aside any future we'd have in Michigan and going off toward things we didn't even know about. And it might not be much of any future at all, if we didn't make it on the trail. Some don't make it, we knew, on account of bad luck, sickness, or Indians. It's a long, hard way, and a lot of things can happen.

You might wonder why I even wanted to

Mona Exinger

go, if I had so many doubts. But Oregon fever is a funny thing – some folks catch it, and some don't. For the ones who do, like me, I guess it's more of an itch than a fever. And once you get the itch, there's nothing to do but scratch it. I knew what our future would be like if we stayed on our farm in Michigan but hadn't the faintest idea of what would happen if we went to Oregon. It sounds scary, but sometimes not knowing is the very thing that'll make you do something. If you don't do it, you'll always wonder – you know that for sure. And me? I can't stand the wondering.

Chapter Two

February

February 11 –

No, I didn't forget about this diary. But the last few months have gone by fast enough to make a gal's head spin, and I haven't had a moment's peace to myself, let alone to write anything.

We've had to bustle around all winter getting ready to go, and that helped make peace in the family again, as everybody pitched in to help. The menfolk helped Marcus make extra axe handles and check all his tools and every inch of harness twice, to make sure everything was as strong as could be. The women had a quilting bee for me at Mary Ann's and made a friendship quilt I'll treasure

Home on the Trail

forever. Each made a square of her own choosing and put her name on it. I know the caring that was put in the stitches will keep us mighty warm.

But even with all the help, what a lot of work! My fingers flew with the extra spinning and weaving and knitting and sewing, making clothes and sacks and bedding – although it's not the way I like to work, all in a huff and hurry.

Those are more restful tasks, like you ought to do of an evening when children are in bed and all's quiet, not be rushing to do them in the middle of the day when everyone's about. Then you're telling Hester to get her fingers out of the stewpot, wiping ash off Matthew's face, when Marcus comes in to say, "We might have to get a new plow, and I'm hungry, where's lunch?" Right about then I'd like to say, "I don't know – where is lunch? I'm hungry, too." Flusters a body's mind some, I can tell you.

February 23 –

Got a fair price for the farm from Robert, and we had a bit more put by, but did it ever cost to get everything we needed!

Marcus and I sat at the table after supper every night for a week, planning out a list of

Mona Exinger

all we should take, and it was a lot. We got a new wagon, big and strong, and a team of oxen – Bob and Bert, their names are – that Marcus had his eye on to buy from Mr. Overton west of town. There were barrels and kegs and boxes and sacks of flour, meal, salt pork, coffee, beans, tools, clothing, pots.

We need enough to keep going for half a year of traveling and to start up again in Oregon when we get there. But when we brought the supplies home from the mercantile and piled them in the barn with everything else we'd gathered together, it looked like we'd be feeding an army instead of a family.

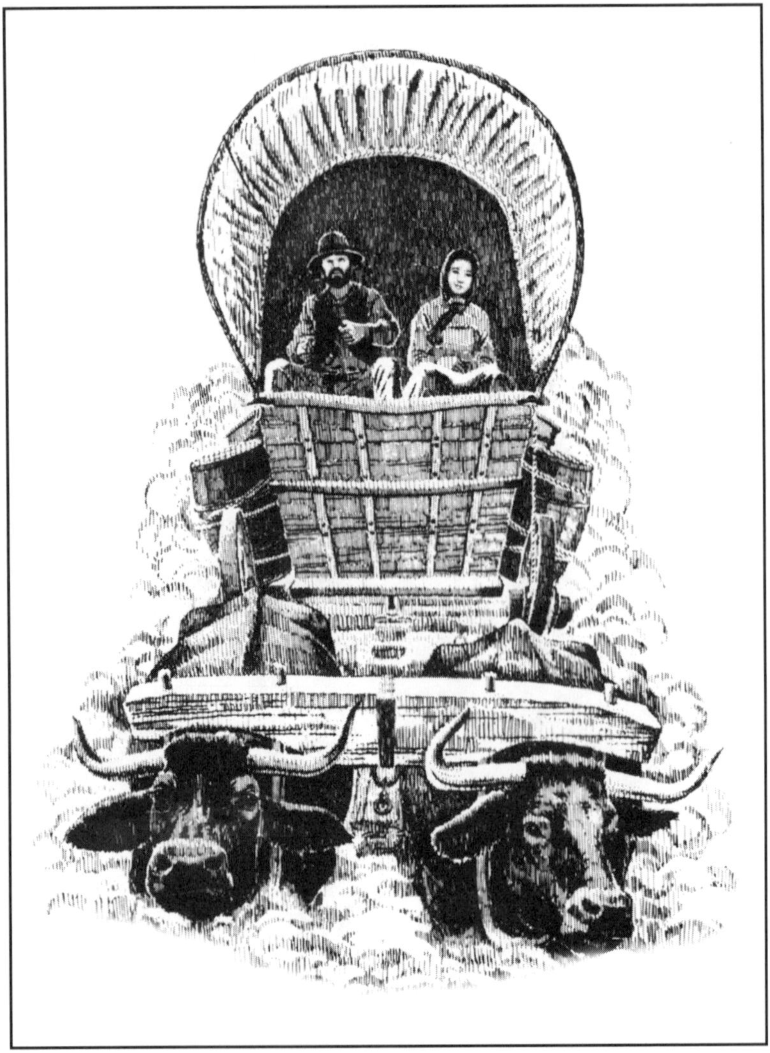

Chapter Three

March

March 8 –

Marcus is handy at more things than I can keep track of, and all this readying for the trip he called outfitting ourselves. That's what happened, all right; he's been out fitting up that brand-new wagon every night for two weeks. Everything had to fit in or out just so, and he made sure it did. Boxes were nailed down, kegs wedged in, the churn roped on, and sacks hung from the wagon-bows overhead. I shake my head in wonder at the smart things he comes up with, and since Marcus is so quick with almost everything, I've done a lot of head-shaking lately.

You know, it's a funny thing – when he

Home on the Trail

brought it home, that wagon looked so big I didn't think we could ever fill it up. But after he started loading it with the pile of supplies we had in the barn, that wagon just started looking smaller all the time.

March 12 –

Tomorrow is Robert and Eleanor's wedding, and I'm glad we can see it before we leave in a few days. Along with lots of other folks, both our families'll be there – making it our last gathering – and there ought to be some real toe-stomping when Marcus' brother Joseph gets out his fiddle. I'm glad we'll have a chance to say goodbye in the middle of a happy event. That should cheer us on our way, instead of making a teary time of it, which is a risk for me, sure enough.

Ma slipped over to see me yesterday and brought her best china teapot, so we had ourselves a private little tea party. She said she felt bad for being cross at that Sunday dinner way back, but it's just that she was taken so hard by the idea of us leaving. I said it was no matter, since she'd always told me herself that a body can't hang onto what folks say when they're angry, else we'd each have a pile of regrets shoulder-high sitting nearby.

The tears flowed as freely as the tea at that

Mona Exinger

party, since that was the real leave-taking between the two of us, saying what was in our hearts. Now we can be brave in front of the rest of the family when it comes time to get in the wagon and go.

March 15 –

Left early this morning with snow still all over the ground.

Spring doesn't come soon in Michigan, and we have to make it to a place far away called Independence in time to catch the rest of our wagon train. Mr. Bates had already gone on ahead with his family, and he told us how to get there and when to meet him.

All the folks had gathered before sunup to see us off, and I knew those hugs and kisses would have to last me a long time. As we went down our old familiar road once more, we all looked back and waved – me for the longest – while I painted the picture into my memory. I know Robert and Eleanor will be happy and keep the farm real well, but I wish I could be here to see it. I didn't cry for fear the tears would freeze on my face.

Guess I'll have to learn to do my diary-writing in the wagon and with my mittens on. Bumps and jolts and cold fingers might not make it too easy to read, but I'll do my best.

Home on the Trail

March 25 –

We'd taken the road to Chicago, a good one, and still frozen hard, making for better traveling. Marcus got used to driving Bob and Bert, or maybe they all got used to each other. Seemed odd not to have our old smaller wagon and be driving the roan. We left him warm and safe in Robert and Eleanor's barn. It was so cold I took turns holding each of the children right up next to me, with the friendship quilt wrapped around both of us to keep warm.

I'd never seen any of Illinois country before, but their farms and towns looked a lot like what we had in Michigan, so I was glad not to feel too strange. Chicago is the biggest town I've ever seen, loud and rowdy, and I was satisfied to keep on moving and leave it behind us.

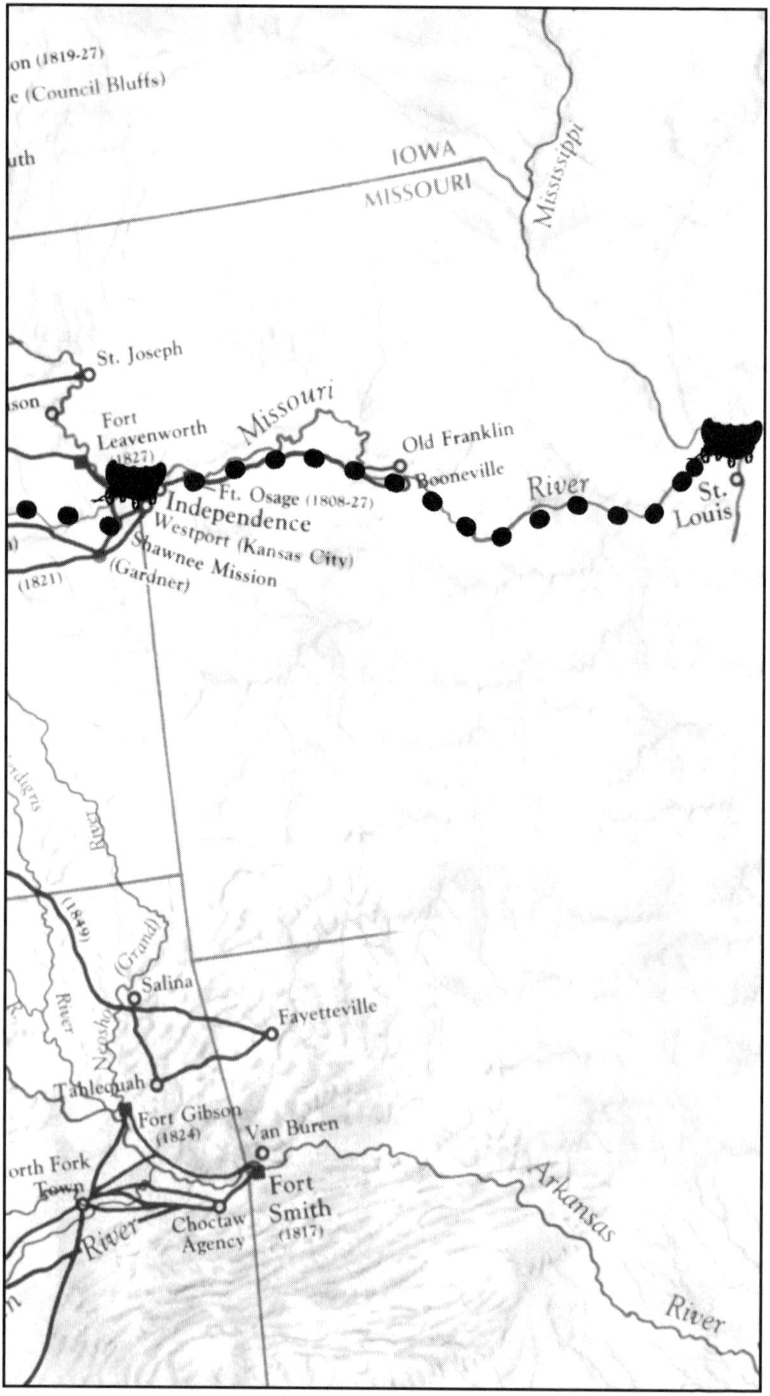

on (1819-27)
e (Council Bluffs)
uth
IOWA
MISSOURI
Mississippi
St. Joseph
son
Fort
Leavenworth
(1827)
Missouri
Old Franklin
Booneville
Ft. Osage (1808-27)
Independence
Westport (Kansas City)
Shawnee Mission
(Gardner)
(1821)
River
St.
Louis
River
(1849)
(Grand)
Salina
Fayetteville
River
Neosho
Tahlequah
Fort Gibson
(1824)
Van Buren
orth Fork
Town
Fort
Smith
(1817)
Choctaw
Agency
River
Arkansas
River

Chapter Four

April

April 7 –

Snow and cold lasted a long time, which was hard on our fingers and toes, but lucky for the road, which hasn't been muddy until the last couple of days, just before we got into the town of Nauvoo. We're still in Illinois, but we've traveled a long way already – and I keep telling myself not to get discouraged yet. This is only the beginning.

April 10 –

Guess I'll learn not to complain about traveling on a road. Here we are in St. Louis, and you'll never believe it, but we got here by

Home on the Trail

floating down the Mississippi River on a raft. Now that was something!

Back up at Nauvoo, Marcus drove the ox team and wagon right up onto a big raft made of logs. Thinking about how heavy the wagon was, I just knew we would sink. But we didn't. It was the oddest feeling, with the water moving right underneath the logs, like you were half-standing, half-swimming. I couldn't hardly stand up for my jelly knees. I was still so scared we would sink, that I clung to the little ones so tight they began squealing in complaint.

After a while it wasn't so bad, and I loosened my grip on the children a bit. But I warned them to pay me strict mind, else they might wind up in the water, unexpected-like. I feared none of us were strong enough swimmers to hold our own in a river this big.

We looked around at what was going by on the banks alongside, and it was real curious to see folks going about their business as usual, with us floating by, just watching it all.

April 13 –

Independence – it's what we've got and the name of the town.

Folks here say it's a proper name for a jumping-off place on the long trail to Oregon.

Mona Exinger

That's likely true, but I'd say we did our jumping off quite a ways back in Michigan.

To make it here from St. Louis, we had to get on another big raft and come up the Missouri River. But this time the raft was steam-powered, and that made more smoke and noise than I hope to see and hear again for a long time. I told Marcus I thought we were driving to Oregon, not sailing. No rest for the wicked, he told me.

I was glad enough to be back up on dry land here in Independence, and I'm almost looking forward to lots of traveling on land, even though people say there's still more rivers to cross along the way. Hope I don't get those jelly knees again.

We met up with Mr. Bates right where he said he'd be, which is a good sign to me that he's the reliable sort. He's got everyone gathered together in a camp east of town until we leave in a few days, so it's an opportunity to meet some of the other folks and make double-sure we have everything we need. Marcus got out his tattered old list of our supplies and checked it again, once by himself and then again with Mr. Bates, to ask him if we'd planned wisely. Mr. Bates looked our wagon over and said we'd done a fine job, and smart folks like us were the kind he'd need to count on along the trail. I agree.

Home on the Trail

After supper I did a little visiting around and met a woman named Susannah Marker, who seems a kind and sensible sort, another one of those smart folks. She and her son and husband came from down in Ohio, just below the Michigan border. Mrs. Marker and I had a good talk, and I like her. I hope she likes me, too. It wouldn't be so lonely traveling such a long way if you had a friend to talk with.

April 15 –

So there we were today, finally leaving Independence and jumping off onto the Oregon Trail. Two dozen wagons our train has, and well over a hundred people – enough for a town. Most wagons have whole families, a few have just single men. We looked pretty important, all hitched up to go. Mr. Bates – we call him Cyrus now – went around and checked on everyone twice before he gave the signal to go. All of us were so excited we could hardly stand waiting.

Independence is a busy town, with people always coming and going from somewhere to somewhere, and we drove from our camp right through town, the townsfolk watching the whole train leave. They waved and cheered us on and yelled good luck. Made me feel proud to be a part of such a thing.

Mona Exinger

April 23 –

The most important thing that happened during the first days on the trail was getting set in our everyday pattern of doing things. Everybody gets up before the sun, men seeing to animals and tightening up on wagons, women getting fires back up and fixing breakfast, children doing their trail chores. One of their chores is something we women wind up doing, too, and I never could have seen myself doing it at home. When I tell you, you might think I made it up, but trail ways are different, and we just have to get used to them.

They call this land out here the prairie or the plains, because that's exactly what it is: plain land. There are hardly any trees, and where there are any, they're only small ones. So what we use for fires is to burn what we politely say are buffalo chips. Marcus played the fool and said it's a dung good thing those buffalo were generous and left them behind for us. I gave him a hard look.

But these chips burn pretty well, and that's all we have, so once you get used to the idea, you say to yourself that's trail ways, and be done with it. Mrs. Wickham, one of the women I've met, says that's part of the God-will-provide part you're always told about in

Home on the Trail

the Bible. It never says what He will provide, just that He will. Some places I've noticed the Bible is real detailed and others not as much. The chips are right along and around the trail, so I guess God provided in the right place, anyway. You walk along and pick them up and store them in your apron or in an old sack, so by the time of the next meal, you've got what you need for your fire.

The meals aren't much to write home about, so I'll just keep it here instead. Plain food is what we get on the plains and everywhere else we'll be going: mostly salt pork, bread or biscuits, and coffee – sometimes beans, but we try to save those.

Every once in a while, when they get itchy for something to do, more than for any other reason, some of the men'll go off a little way and do what they call hunting. I don't call it that, because what they mostly bring back is nothing. Marcus is a good shot, but by the time he gets a rabbit out here, he's spent quite a few bullets. I say nothing about the bullets. At least I say nothing loud enough for the neighbors to hear, then I stew up the rabbit and try to make it last us as long as I can.

I sorely miss potatoes or any other kind of vegetable. There was no sense bringing any, they'd just go bad. The only way to do it would be in a barrel of sand, and that's too

Mona Exinger

much weight in the wagon. It'll be a long spell before we get a garden planted in Oregon and taste good fresh things again. I try not to think how long, but it's hard when you're starting out and the meals get tiresome already. What I wouldn't give for a meal like the one at Robert and Eleanor's wedding – fried chicken, potato salad, pickles, apple bread, and cakes and pies 'til the cows come home. Well, wishing won't make it happen.

One thing I did was tuck away some dried apples and pumpkin pieces when I packed our food, and glad enough we are for them now, too. I might slip in a few apples to fry with the salt pork or mix into the biscuits every now and then to add flavor. The pumpkin you have to soak more, so that goes in as a treat when we have beans or stew. Some of the train folks haven't such things, and that's another reason to kind of disguise them in the food, so we don't look like we're glorifying what we've got and they don't. Either they didn't plan ahead as well, or didn't have a farm back home to take from, or couldn't afford to buy any.

In the beginning, it rankled me not to be friendly and share what we had with others, but Marcus had the wise word on that. He said some of the folks were foolish enough to

Home on the Trail

come ill-prepared, even when we all knew it'd be a long, hard trip. There'll be plenty of time to share later, after those folks have done their best to eke out what they brought. Marcus didn't mean it in a selfish or unkind manner, just as a way of looking ahead and being there for folks after they've tried their best, and maybe it wasn't enough. He's what you'd call a farsighted man, and he thinks of these things other people don't.

We always set out early to start getting the miles under our belts. It's still cold in the morning, but warms as the day wears on, and you feel warmer once you get moving. Most of us walk along by our wagons instead of riding, since you don't want to make things any heavier for your team than need be. Old people sometimes ride, or children, when they get tired, or somebody who's sick.

I thought the trail would be like a road where the leader would be in front and the rest following behind in a line, but that's not the way it is at all. The Bates wagon is in front, with one of Cyrus' boys driving, but the rest of us are all spread out over the land, so as not to choke in each other's dust. Choking in your own dust is plenty by itself. Cyrus himself stays in front for a while, telling his boy things to watch out for to stay in the right direction, then he rides back among the

Mona Exinger

rest of us to see who's lagging or might be broken down. He's the only man in the train who rides – the rest of them walk, leading their ox or mule teams – but I can't envy him even for that. With all the backtracking and circling he's got to do, he goes twice as far as the rest of us in any one day.

People are fresher in the morning, so they tend to talk more and be friendlier to each other. It's not too long before you start telling about family and friends, all the things you left back home and the reasons you're going to Oregon. It's interesting to listen to other folks and trade tales back and forth. Lots of little things make us see we have more in common than we might have thought before.

The men are the ones full of dreams and plans about how it's going to be, and what they're going to do and have when we get there. Women talk to each other about people and homes they left behind, how they miss them already and whether it will ever be the same anywhere else.

They talk of what their gardens grew and the seeds they brought along to make new gardens. And of course, they talk about food. Trading receipts makes for some important discussions. You'll come up behind two or three women holding forth, and sure enough, one's bound to be saying, "Well, the

Home on the Trail

way I do it is add just an extra pinch of saleratus, and they turn out light as a feather. It's the way my ma always taught me." Maybe the reason women converse on food so much is the fact that it's so plain on the trail, and we're all looking forward to cakes and vegetables and other good things when we get our Oregon homes set up and settled into.

So after talking of food and other things all morning while walking, we stop for our same old lunch of biscuit, salt pork and coffee. It's a quick rest, only an hour or so – hardly time to make a fire to fry our pork and heat water for coffee. Fortunately, we've got our fire fixings all ready, having been gathering those buffalo chips all morning while trading receipts. Not such a pleasant twosome to think about together, but the talking does help to pass the time, and we need the chips for the lunch fires, so at least it's all rolled together in a practical way.

After lunch, we get on the move again and walk all afternoon.

This isn't as much of a talkative time, and less so as the day wears on, since everyone's getting tired. It's when each of us has time to think to ourselves about how big a thing it is we're doing and how much change it'll bring to our lives. You look around at the land and wonder how it would be to live someplace here along the way and what Oregon is really like.

Finally we stop in the early evening. After being spread out on the trail all day, we gather our wagons closer together, and people get settled in for the night. Horses and mules have to be picketed so they don't wander. The oxen and the few cattle folks brought just stay together by themselves, but a man named Harve Drucker has an extra-mean old bull that has to be tied up a way off, so as not to cause undue trouble. Men look over any problems with the wagons and get together with Cyrus on where the next day's travel will take us. We women busy ourselves with getting supper and making room in the wagons for putting children to bed later.

Susannah Marker, the woman I met the first night in Independence, has a boy, Johnny, two years older than our Matt. Johnny is just the one for a game anytime, so he always gets the rest of the boys going in something. If you listen to them, it sounds like there's an awful lot of odd rules that keep changing, depending on who has the ball and what he thinks about it. So there's about as much talking and arguing going on as there is playing the game. They'll grow up to be men, that's for sure.

Girls gather with their dolls and have a social time when they can, which is whenever they're not busy helping with dinner or

Home on the Trail

watching little brothers and sisters. (Guess that means they'll grow up to be busy women, just like their mas.)

Blankets come out for a man or an older boy to sleep under the wagon, or to wrap up in while taking their turn at the watch. Marcus takes his turn as regular as the others, but of course Matt's too little. He sleeps in the wagon with Hester and me. Not too long after supper, the children are put to bed. Then there's a bit of grown-up time, while women do dishes and men rest or check the animals again.

If you're lucky, maybe there's a few minutes to sit peacefully with your husband and talk quietly about your future before turning in for the night. Marcus gets more peace than talk on the nights I write in this diary, and he had a lot of peace tonight.

When you finally get to bed, it's so quiet you can hear all sorts of odd night noises around you on the prairie, but it's only a few minutes before you're sound asleep. All of our busyness makes for a long day, and most of them will probably be the same.

April 30 –

Well, we hadn't gone very far from Independence before some of our train realized they should have listened to what they were told about not packing too much. Some folks overloaded their wagons something fierce with things they thought they just couldn't leave behind. I'll be honest on this: Mostly it was the women who couldn't bear to leave their nice furniture pieces and gewgaws, but a few of the men got carried away and brought an extra anvil or plow or something. The poor teams pulling these wagons could hardly do it on flat land. We have a long, long way to go, then come mountains which are supposed to be taller than anything we've ever seen. Some of these people were so loaded, you wouldn't think they'd make it to the next river.

    Finally, Cyrus got pretty tough with these folks and said they had to start tossing things out to lighten their wagons, or they'd fall behind the rest of us, and he wouldn't be responsible. Some argued and said they wouldn't do it, but after a few days of lagging behind and having their teams worn out all the time, they saw the light and unloaded some. It looked mighty peculiar to see a chest of drawers sitting out here in the middle of the outdoors, being left behind as we moved along. Something like that looks lonely, like it's just waiting for somebody else to come along and take it in.

Home on the Trail

One woman – Clara McCreedy, I believe her name is – raised a terrible ruckus about a chest of her grandmother's she didn't want to leave behind. It was huge, and must have weighed a ton. I thought I could hear their mule team heave a sigh of relief when it was unloaded. Clara was standing by, wringing her hands, crying (much more noise than tears, so you know what that means), and near cursing out Cyrus for making her husband do it. The husband wasn't crying any, I might add, but that woman'll be trouble, I can tell already.

She said people coming along behind us would load that chest right up and take it with them to Oregon, and if she ever walked into someone's house out there and saw they had what she knew was hers, she'd have the law on them in no time. Marcus turned away so she couldn't see, then chuckled and said who would be fool enough to come along and take Clara's chest on their wagon, when they'll probably be unloading their own things along here somewhere, too? Besides, good luck to her finding the law in Oregon, where there really isn't much yet.

I was glad we had planned better and made our hard choices way back in Michigan on what to take along. By this time, my grieving for things we left behind was long since over. And what's more, my furniture has a good home, keeping Robert and Eleanor company, so it's not out here getting lonely on the trail.

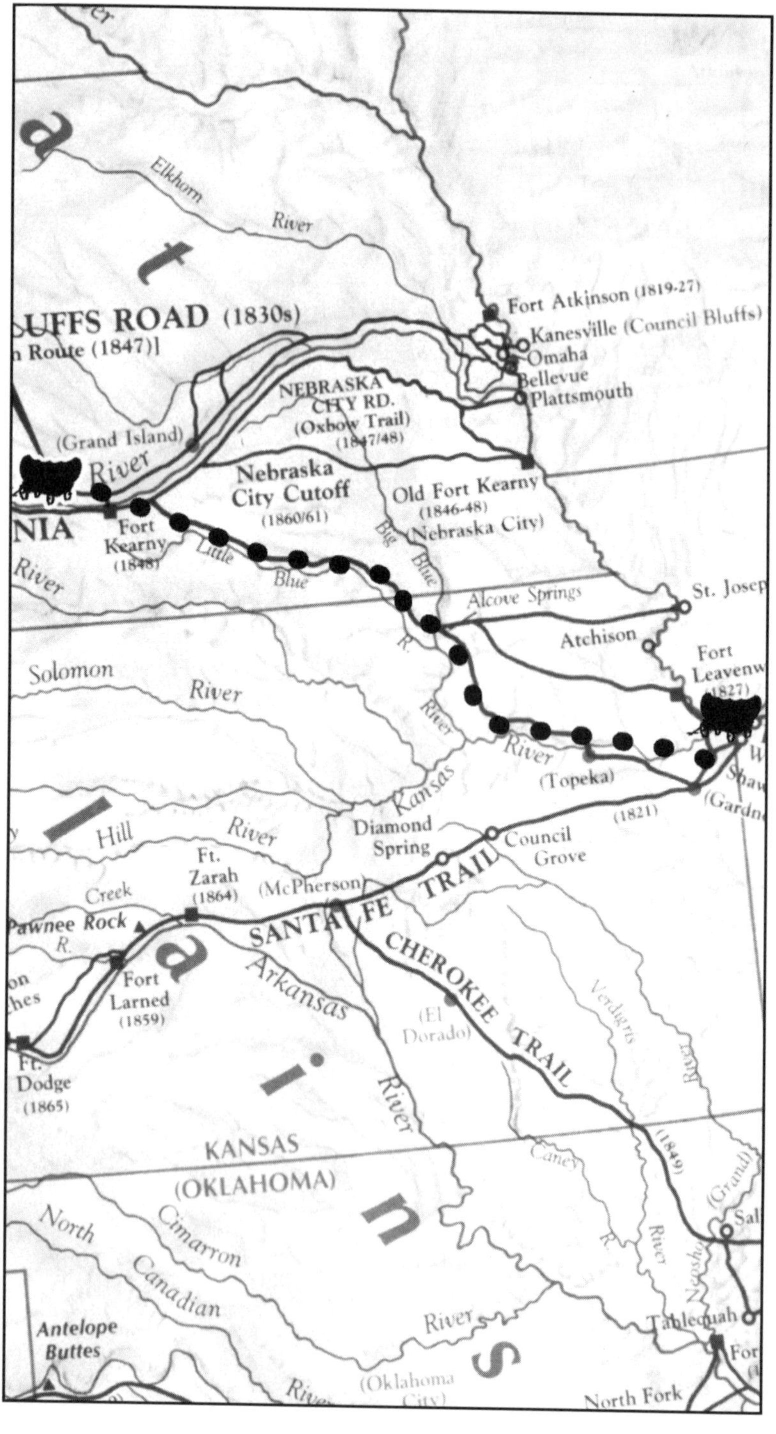

UFFS ROAD (1830s)
n Route (1847)]
Elkhorn
River
Fort Atkinson (1819-27)
Kanesville (Council Bluffs)
Omaha
Bellevue
Plattsmouth
NEBRASKA CITY RD. (Oxbow Trail) (1847/48)
(Grand Island)
River
Nebraska City Cutoff (1860/61)
Old Fort Kearny (1846-48) (Nebraska City)
NIA
Fort Kearny (1848)
Little Blue
Big Blue
River
Alcove Springs
St. Josep
Atchison
Fort Leavenw (1827)
R.
Solomon
River
River
River
(Topeka)
Kansas
(1821)
(Gardn
Hill
River
Diamond Spring
Council Grove
Ft. Zarah (1864)
(McPherson)
Creek
Pawnee Rock
R.
SANTA FE TRAIL
CHEROKEE TRAIL
Fort Larned (1859)
Arkansas
(El Dorado)
Verdigris
River
Ft. Dodge (1865)
River
(1849)
KANSAS
(OKLAHOMA)
(Grand)
North
Cimarron
Caney
R.
River
Neosho
Canadian
River
Tahlequah
Antelope Buttes
(Oklahoma City)
North Fork

Chapter Five

May

May 7 –

Just put the children to bed for the night, which makes me want to brag a bit about the way they've both behaved on the trail. I'll say out loud I'm proud to be their ma. Our Hester and Matthew walk right along with a good will and are always looking around and interested in things. I told them they'd best keep a sharp lookout, because this would be one of the great events of their lives. Seems most of the grown-ups have their minds so set on Oregon, that's all they think about. They don't enjoy things along the way, like the children do.

Traveling on the trail is hard for anyone –

Home on the Trail

and harder on children. It's all walking and not much play, except at night when you're almost too tired to do it. It was cold at first, and we had to walk bundled up in all of our shawls and coats, looking like a bunch of clothes heaps rolling along the trail. That made for some heavy going, especially for those not so tall. But now the days are warming up, and we don't need to wear as many layers. You can move your arms and legs a bit more freely, and I've noticed hopping and skipping are on the rise.

While our family's not rich and can't afford lots of toys for our little ones, we make do in simpler ways. Hester has a new doll I made before we left, so she'd be fresh for the trip. It's only a sock doll, but it has a cheery face sewed on and not one but two dresses. There's nothing wrong with being fashionable on the trail. That doll is pretty loved, I'd say, and kept real clean, considering we live outside all the time.

All of life's an adventure to Matt, and his toys are less lasting. They're either some little thing his pa's carved after supper that gets lost the next day – Marcus learned not to spend too much time on these after the first three or four – or sticks or rocks he picks up along the way that he pretends are spears or cannonballs. It's even harder to keep Matt clean on the trail than it was at home, but he keeps happy, and that's probably better in the long run than staying clean.

We all play games as we walk along, like who can find six different flowers before lunch, who can see a bird first, or who can tell the best story of what Oregon'll be like when we get there. I always think the children take after Marcus in being so smart. Who knows what they got from me?

May 13 –

Getting to know people in the train is so interesting. It takes a bit of the sting out of missing folks at home. We never even met these people until a few weeks ago, and there are so many of them – more than a hundred – I was sure I couldn't begin to remember all their names. I'm not so quick at that as some.

But here you are, tossed together all the time, having to help each other do things like hitch up, gather buffalo chips, and watch out for the little ones. So, before you know it, you're calling to Deborah that you scrabbled up a button from your workbasket that might come close to matching the one Katie lost off her dress yesterday. Or you're asking Sarah Ann if she'll watch your boy while you walk back a few wagons to ask after somebody's mother who was ailing this morning.

It's a friendly crowd for the most part,

Home on the Trail

since we all have in common the fact we've pulled up our roots to take them across the country and plant them down again in Oregon. I've met nearly everybody, and while most I just wave and smile to, some are on the way to being friends already.

Susannah is the one I like best. She and her husband Ethan did all right on their farm in Ohio, but like us, they decided to give Oregon a try. Their son Johnny is smart as a whip and full of ideas. Susannah said he'd already read the few books in their school back home, so I told her I'd ask Marcus about digging out some of his for Johnny to borrow while we're on the trail.

Mrs. Wickham is a widow woman traveling with her son Nathan, a strong boy of about twenty, who takes good care of his ma. A lot of women, once they're widowed, turn what I call namby-pamby – they're always after folks to feel sorry for them and do for them. But Mrs. Wickham has more sense than any five women you could pick and never lets this widowhood pull her down. She thought nothing of leaving her farm and going all the way to Oregon on her own with her son, once she determined there was a chance they might do better there.

Then there's the Cogburns, with their oldest daughter Lacey and a herd of younger ones, running down in age like stairsteps.

Mona Exinger

Lacey's sixteen and knows what she wants already – that being Nathan Wickham. Once she set eyes on that boy, it was all over for him, although he doesn't know it yet. Half a dozen times a day, she'll find some excuse to flounce over to where he's leading his team and make conversation. But it isn't long before one of her sisters comes running for her. Mr. Cogburn looks to be a stern sort, who doesn't approve of Lacey's waving herself in the breeze like that. My guess is the two of them will have it out before the trip to Oregon is over. And with all those girls, Lacey'll only be the first of his battles.

Another man without a moment's peace is Cyrus Bates. Being our leader is surely a thankless task, but he doesn't complain. His wife is raising a passel of sturdy boys, and I asked her once if she'd trade for one of the Cogburns' girls. She laughed and said not likely, as even with all the slingshot and buckshot and falling out of trees she's had to put up with, she still thinks boys are less trouble. From what I've seen myself, I believe Mr. Cogburn would agree.

Harve and Nancy Drucker are another couple I've met, and they're traveling with old Mrs. Drucker, Harve's ma. Harve says his bull – the mean one we've got to be careful of – is only as wicked as he is himself. But that couldn't be further from the truth. Harve's a

Home on the Trail

fun-loving man with a grin on his face, and his wife, Nancy, is a strong, feisty gal with life firmly in hand. Her children are always polite and quick with a "yes, ma'am" or "yes, sir," and she can tell you exactly what's where in every inch of her wagon. Mrs. Drucker finds no fault with such a daughter-in-law, I'm sure.

Then there's the McCreedys, who aren't friends, but I might mention them, anyway. Clara's the one who whined so about tossing things out along the trail that she shouldn't have brought anyway. And that was only the beginning. She's always got a sharp word to say about anyone and is making such a bad time of this traveling, it's a wonder she came at all – unless her town back East talked her into it for their own sake. I don't suppose I've heard Mr. McCreedy say more than a dozen words, but it isn't as if he gets a chance. Marcus said maybe he's deaf, and I said no, that couldn't be, for when I spoke to him he heard me fine. Then Marcus just smiled.

May 18 –

Here we are traveling alongside the Platte River. They say Platte means flat in somebody's language; it sure is that, and wide. It's shallow, too, but the water's not clean enough to look down into. And there are lots

Mona Exinger

of bugs, since the river moves so slowly. It practically stands in one place. The Platte will be our traveling companion for quite some time.

After we went along by the river a short way, we came to Fort Kearney, which wasn't much of a fort to my taste – meaning I wouldn't feel too safe holed up here if some Indians were to group up all of a sudden. Makes me wonder how it'll be way out on the trail, without even a shabby excuse like this to hide behind. Haven't seen any Indians yet, and it'd suit me if we didn't – except maybe one, just to look at. One wouldn't be able to group up and scare a body.

Anyway, Fort Kearney did have a blacksmith to make repairs to wagons that were showing signs of wear already. It's not a good sign for those folks, and I'm not too proud to say we weren't among them. Marcus has seen to it our wagon's still sturdy and tightly packed.

At the fort, we rested a day – well, not exactly what I'd call a rest, only a different kind of work – but we didn't move on the trail, so that was something. The women did laundry, and we were glad to have the chance, too. Guess these chances don't come often on the trail. The children rested enough to get sassy again.

After the laundry was set out to dry, some

Home on the Trail

women were all in a fuss about buying more supplies here at the fort, so I went along just to see. One look at the prices that storekeeper charged, and I was out of there in a hurry. Ought to be a law against charging people like that! His stock was so poor, and no choice amongst it. He should have been ashamed. I'd think he couldn't do business in a proper town, since nobody'd ever come back again. He had to set up shop out here where people only go through once, and he doesn't have to fear a snubbing at church for being so greedy with his prices.

But I'm never one to waste time, I hope, so I wrote some letters to the family back home, while the foolish women did their marketing. I miss my folks, of course, and Mary Ann something fierce, and I wonder how Robert and Eleanor are coming along with the farm. But we can't expect any letters in return for a long time – probably not until we get to Oregon and stay in one spot. There's nothing to do but keep writing and hope they'll understand.

I spoke to Mrs. Bates yesterday about her son Rafe. He's the oldest, who went out with Cyrus before and is still in Oregon, getting their farm going. She hasn't seen him in two years and misses him sorely. It's hard not to get any word at all on how your loved ones are. My letters were a quick work and none too neat, but the folks ought to be glad to know we've made it this far in one piece.

Another thing I can say about the land around the Platte: With water so close, you'd never think it could be so dry. The dust is just everywhere! We dragged into the fort looking like a crowd of clay figures – people, clothes, animals, wagons – all covered with the same dull, brown dust. Doing our laundry only lessened it a bit.

I'm too busy at home to waste time polishing much, and I don't have any silver or that kind of fancy thing, but I always thought I was a clean soul about my house. I didn't want to tolerate too much dirt on the trail, and somehow I figured there'd be ample chance for that, what with traveling for months and months. So I sewed three sets of flour and meal bags – to keep each inside the other – instead of one set, like most gals. And I'd say it paid off, as I believe now I have less bugs and dirt in my flour and meal than most of the women do.

It sounds awful, but everybody has bugs and dirt that have settled in, and there's nothing to do but put up with it. Laurella Atkins, a woman whose wagon always pokes along at the end of our train, only sewed one set, and poor cloth it was, too. Her family can hardly eat the bread she makes without it being mostly dirt.

I saw her bags and thought to myself,

Home on the Trail

"What can she expect, after using such cloth? You can practically see through it, the weaving is so loose." It's that real cheap stuff the storekeeper back home likes to get rid of, but he didn't sell it to me, because I wouldn't have any part of that nonsense, and he knew it. I never said anything to Laurella about it, though. I am more of a Christian woman than to rub her face in the dirt – as there's enough in her bread already.

May 20 –

One of the Huggins boys got bit by a rattlesnake yesterday and suffered hard for a night, then died. He was playing along the trail in the grass away from the wagons, the way Hester and Matthew do, but maybe a little farther out. Such a sorrow to come when all we're trying to do is get to a new home! And everyone had tried to be so careful about the children and the wagons, since a dreadful thing that sometimes happens is that a child'll fall out of a wagon and be crushed under the wheels. It's something we women didn't want to think about, but did, enough to keep our caution with us.

Mr. Huggins, the boy's father, is a man who looks cross and says little. Makes me think the family had to come out West because there was some trouble back home.

Mona Exinger

That's the way it is with some folks, running away. I'd rather think our family's running to something, instead of the other.

It was hard on everybody to think of a child fading away so quick like that – as careless as you'd blow out a candle – but it was worst on his ma. Poor Ruth Huggins is a thin, tired-looking rail of a woman, dragged along on the trail by her husband. She has six children and another on the way, and she's younger than me, though she looks worn.

Mrs. Bates, Cyrus' wife, was a midwife back home and has some knowledge of sickness and such, so she went to take a look at the boy. But she came away with her lips tight, shaking her head. The rest of us women went a few at a time, to sit through the night with Ruth and her son Jake. There was nothing else we could do, and we knew it.

Clara McCreedy said it hardly mattered, that Ruth's one on the way would just take the place of the other child, and that such folks are a waste and no good to begin with. I was shocked and tried to shush her. Mrs. Wickham let loose and said, "Shut up!" and nearly slapped her. Shush or shut up, Clara did it. Thank the Lord – and I did – that Ruth heard none of it. I went back to our wagon after my turn, laid right down by my little Matt and held him in his sleep, I was so grateful to have him safe.

Home on the Trail

In the morning, poor Jake was dead. Susannah gave a quilt to wrap him in, and we had a little burying service. We knew the boy'd die, so during the night Susannah had set her husband, Ethan, to make a cross out of part of a box, and carve on it Jake's name and the date. It probably wasn't easy work to take the box apart and do all that quietly in the middle of the night, so the Hugginses wouldn't be reminded what was going to happen. But Ethan had done it, and we'd never heard a sound.

Ruth had sat with Jake all through the night and hadn't cried, but she cried some now. Mr. Huggins looked crosser than ever, but I think he was just sad. The rest of the Huggins children were as quiet as mice, and some of the women took them in hand for the day to keep them out of Ruth's way and let her grieve in peace.

The worst part was after the burying. Really, it was two things. First of all, we had to leave and get on the trail again right away to make time. All of us ached in our hearts for Ruth having to leave her child, knowing he'd always be out there apart from her, and she couldn't ever visit the grave or bring flowers. Susannah put Ruth to bed in their wagon and sent it ahead, so she wouldn't see the second awful thing. We had to take some of the other wagons and drive them right over that poor little grave we'd made, to muss it up so wild animals wouldn't get at it. Stirs the dirt up and takes the people-smell away, some of the men said. It seemed an awful savage thing to do, but trail ways are different from regular home ways, and we can never forget it. Finally, we gathered together what few stones we could find and put those on top, with the grave cross Ethan had made. There was nothing else to do after that but move on.

Later in the day, when I saw Ruth walking outside the wagon again, I caught up to her and walked along, holding her hand, to show her I cared and was sorry for her burden.

May 22 –

I'd best tell how the whole wagon train crosses a river. I'm reminded of it since we had a long day going over the Platte today, although we went through some littler ones before.

First off, these western rivers are bigger and wider than the ones back home. Sometimes there's a ferry to cross on, which is both good and bad. The good part is that you can just get on the raft and be hauled across, with somebody else doing the work. The bad part is that some of the ferrymen aren't as careful with your wagon as you would be yourself – they'll get your things wet, or even tip the

Home on the Trail

whole mess over. So you don't save any on the worrying. You still have to do as much of that, either way.

Another bad part is how much they charge. I think hard cash is called that because it's so hard to come by. When you don't have much of it, seeing goodly chunks go out of your hands into the ferryman's is – well, hard. I keep careful track of all we've got and hide it away in a secret place I won't even write down here. Once in a while, when I bellyache about it to Marcus, he just nods his head and says we have to get to Oregon, this is part of how we do it, and I shouldn't concern myself over every little penny. That's just it. The way I see it, there are no little pennies – they're all the same size, and all of them have to be worked for equally hard.

It just goes to show that even though two people are married, they don't always see eye to eye about everything, as Marcus and I could tell you. This makes me think of how Lacey Cogburn moons over Nathan Wickham. She probably thinks that a man and marriage only means a snug cabin with roses in the dooryard. I'll have to remember to tell her there's some pitfalls about the whole thing, too, and maybe she'll hold off on her ideas for a while longer.

Anyway, I was telling about crossing the Platte, which didn't have a ferry to go on.

Mona Exinger

First, we all gather on the near side and bring out the buckets of pitch. While men slather pitch on the wagons so they're as tight against the water as they can be, women rustle around inside and stow things away carefully, so nothing gets too wet if the pitch doesn't hold and some water leaks in. We have to make places for the children to ride in the very center of the wagon, away from the edges so they don't fall out. If they ever went into the water, that would be the end, and something nobody wants to think about.

After all the pitching and stowing are done, the men group into what you'd call posses, and each posse works on taking a wagon across. Some of the women, like me, stay on the seat and hang on to their own teams, but some don't, and a man'll take over. Other men get in the water on horses and go alongside the wagons to help if anything happens – like if your team stops or an ox falls down.

We line up on the near bank a few at a time, drive those wagons straight into the water and head for the other side. I was scared the first time we crossed a river, but you can't let on with children in the wagon. You just do it and act brave. You have more than enough to keep your mind and hands busy, and it's over pretty soon.

The team can walk across on the riverbed

Home on the Trail

if it's shallow, but they have to swim if it gets too deep. Here's where I'm thankful we have Bob and Bert and not mules, as the mules really get ahold of their mulish ways and aren't as agreeable about being in the water as the oxen are. If it's very deep, the team starts swimming, and you can feel the wagon rise up and wiggle underneath you when it floats free of the bottom.

Makes everybody glad to get across and be on firm land again. Of course, you don't always wind up straight across from where you started, but you can neaten up the group again after you're all on the far side. The animals don't seem any more fond of this than I am, although Cyrus says the rivers we've crossed so far aren't bad ones at all – it'll get wilder the farther west we go.

When the first of us get over to the far bank, we start a fire. It takes a long time for the men to help everyone across, so there's a good blaze going by then, and they can dry out and have some hot coffee. The children get a chance to climb out and uncramp their legs from being stuffed in so tight, and the women have to check everything in their wagons to see what got wet.

If you find you've had a leak on something, you might be able to spread it out to dry so it's as good as new, like a quilt. But other things – like a sack of meal – might be ruined for good. You just mourn a little over it, dump it out, and figure you'll be that much lighter going over the mountains.

May 23 –

Buffalo. I've seen them from a distance, and they look like huge, lumpy, mean cattle, and they run around in big, dusty herds. They're supposed to make good eating, but we'll never know about it. The buffalo hunting that our menfolk go off and do every once and again is nothing but a lot of foolishness.

You'd think since all those men do is fuss and argue with each other day and night about how we need to hurry along the trail, they'd have more sense than to stop the whole train for such folly. Especially when all they do is ride around and shoot in the dust – mostly at each other, since nobody can see a hand in front of his face in that mess. Who needs even more dust and dirt to wash out of clothes? There have been three of these so-called hunts so far, and not so much as an inch of meat to show for it. We're still eating salt pork, same as always.

My Aunt Louise always said men are like the boards in life, and women are like the nails. Men are real strong, and it looks like they hold up the house, but it's the really the

Home on the Trail

women, because boards don't stay together by themselves, do they? Men have the job of deciding things and acting important, but we women don't have time for acting important. We just are.

(SOUTH DAKOTA)
NEBRASKA

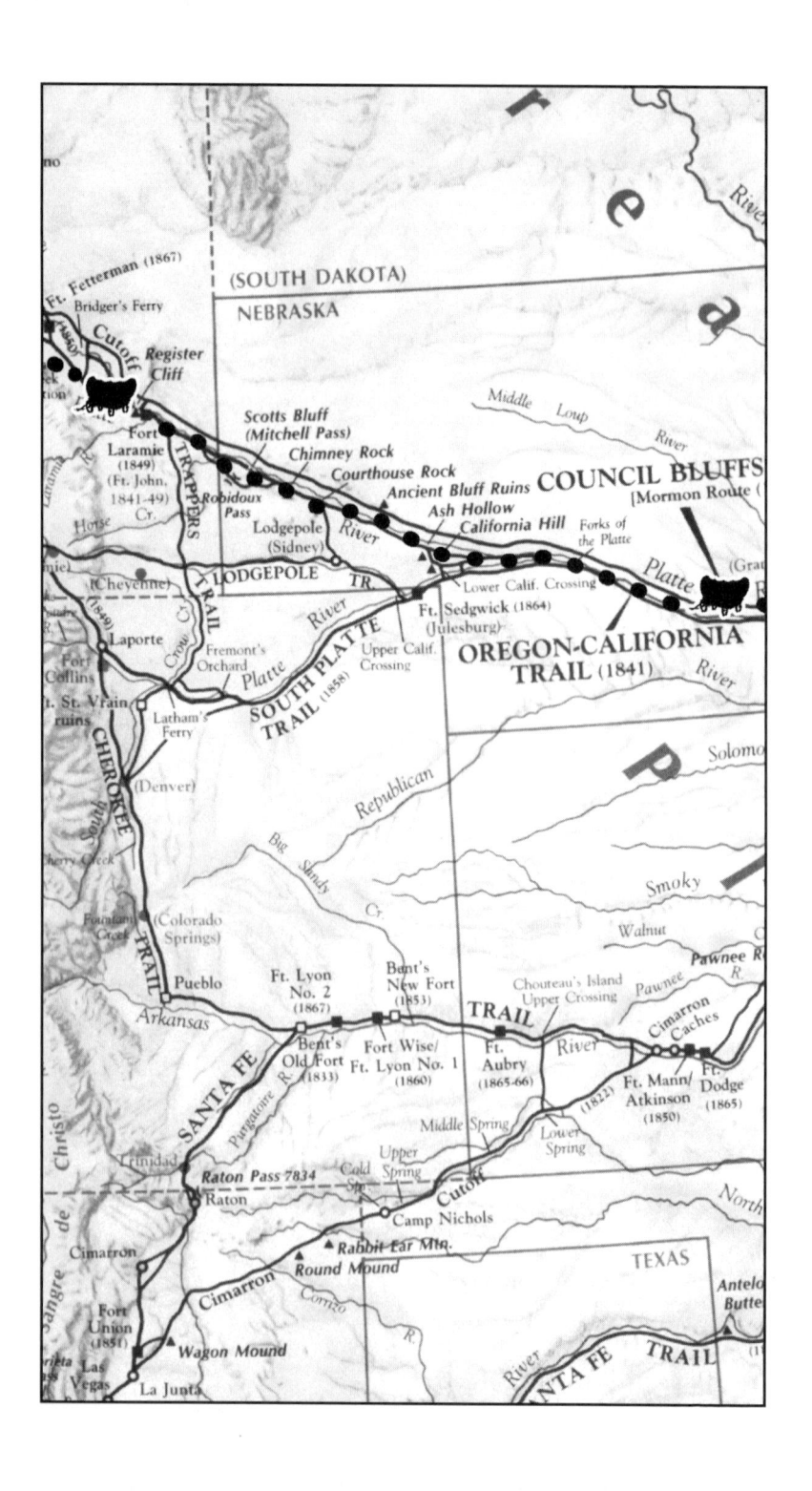

Ft. Fetterman (1867)
Bridger's Ferry
Register Cliff
Scotts Bluff (Mitchell Pass)
Chimney Rock
Courthouse Rock
Ancient Bluff Ruins
Ash Hollow
California Hill
COUNCIL BLUFFS
[Mormon Route]
Fort Laramie (1849) (Ft. John, 1841-49)
Robidoux Pass
Lodgepole (Sidney)
TRAPPERS TRAIL
Middle Loup River
Platte River
Forks of the Platte
(Cheyenne)
LODGEPOLE TR.
Lower Calif. Crossing
Ft. Sedgwick (1864) (Julesburg)
OREGON-CALIFORNIA TRAIL (1841)
Fort Collins
Laporte
Crow Cr.
Fremont's Orchard
Upper Calif. Crossing
SOUTH PLATTE TRAIL (1858)
St. Vrain ruins
Latham's Ferry
South Platte River
CHEROKEE
(Denver)
Republican
Cherry Creek
Solomon
Fountain Creek
(Colorado Springs)
Big Sandy Cr.
Smoky
Walnut
Pawnee R.
Pueblo
Ft. Lyon No. 2 (1867)
Bent's New Fort (1853)
Chouteau's Island Upper Crossing
Pawnee
Cimarron Caches
TRAIL
Arkansas
Bent's Old Fort (1833)
Fort Wise/ Ft. Lyon No. 1 (1860)
Ft. Aubry (1865-66)
River
(1822)
Ft. Mann/ Atkinson (1850)
Ft. Dodge (1865)
SANTA FE
Purgatoire R.
Middle Spring
Lower Spring
Trinidad
Raton Pass 7834
Upper Spring
Cold Sp.
Raton
Cutoff
Camp Nichols
Cimarron
▲ Rabbit Ear Mtn.
Round Mound
TEXAS
Sangre de Cristo
Cimarron
Corrizo R.
North
Fort Union 1851
▲ Wagon Mound
SANTA FE TRAIL
Antelope Butte
Las Vegas
La Junta

Chapter Six

June

June 2 –

Bad times and heartaches hurt even more on the trail, it seems.

You're out here helpless against so many things. There's just no way to escape it. But lately we've had the worst scare since our family started out in Michigan – cholera. It struck the train sudden and hit hard. Maybe anything is hard if you don't expect it and can't do anything about it, except watch folks get sick and die.

One evening, Marcus came back from a meeting with Cyrus and mentioned that Sam Atkins (whose wagon is always last to get ready in the morning and lags behind all day)

Home on the Trail

didn't look too good. Marcus said maybe he'd give Sam a hand hitching up in the morning if he was still feeling poorly, and I said then maybe for once Sam would be on time.

Well, the next morning, Laurella – who is Sam's wife and the one with the dirty bread – went to Cyrus all tearful and said Sam had awful stomach pains and was so sick he couldn't get up. She said she simply couldn't go any farther, as she couldn't lead the team herself. So they'd wind up all alone out here in the middle of nowhere, and whatever was she to do?

Cyrus told Laurella not to worry, that he wasn't about to leave anyone behind. He had his wife go over to check on Sam. Mrs. Bates knew when she looked at him that it was cholera, and that wasn't the best news for the train. Just about the worst possible, as a matter of fact.

Here's one of the times you can tell we made a good deal in finding Cyrus. Some leaders would have been selfish and told Laurella she had to stay behind, seeing as how Sam was too sick to continue. Then they'd have left her there to fend off wolves or Indians or whatever and wouldn't have felt a guilty twinkle ever after.

But Cyrus is an honest man to a fault. He called everyone to a meeting and told us how it was. He said Sam would have to be watched, and we should all be careful and let him know if anyone else got sick. He said he hoped none of us would. Then he asked who'd offer to lead Sam's team. Of course Marcus said he'd do it, and of course he did. But it set us all to worrying as we packed up and started out that day.

We didn't have long to wait before we had to start worrying more. Laurella did everything she could to make her husband comfortable, and Marcus led their team and made her stay inside the wagon all day to care for Sam. But he got worse fast. Sam died about supper time, after we camped. Not only that, but it looked like one of the Atkins children and Laurella had gotten the cholera, and a boy in the Simpson wagon had stomach pains, too.

That was only the beginning. But the next days have been so busy and sad, it's hard to write about them. It happens so fast – you can only stand by and watch more and more folks get sick and take to their wagons. The men and older boys who aren't sick have to double up on chores and leading the teams. They work hard and look tired. The women have it hard, too. We look after children whose parents are ill, cook for everybody, try to mop up after the sick folks and keep as much of the trail dust off them as we can – and warn the men when a grave needs to be dug.

We've done the best we could for the ones who've died, by saying a little service and trying to bury them as properly as you can on the trail. The sickness wasn't only on our train, either. We passed other graves along the way, some saying "died of cholera" on the board or stick that marked them. It pulls at your heart something fierce to see so much grief, but we had to keep on moving, even if it was slower. Caring for the sick was just added to the regular work of trail travel.

The extra work isn't the hardest and most wearing part, though – that's the worry and fear and hoping. There's worry for your family and how much you want to protect them, so they don't get sick, and there's a helpless feeling, knowing you can't do anything – nothing but pray, anyway. Fear seems to make you less human, when folks around you are dying and all you can think about is at least it's the Atkins girl and not your own daughter. You're hoping, always hoping, that you and yours can make it through all in one piece. It doesn't really matter about Oregon anymore, just keeping us alive is the main thought.

We've buried sixteen people from our train along the trail, so their journey is at an end, anyway. And we don't know yet if that'll be all. Some of the families make a sad and holey patchwork of lost husbands, wives, or children. The rest of us are clasping hands, you could say, around those who are left and trying to do for them.

The Brewsters and the Wilburs and the Merrilees have taken in children who've lost their parents. Mrs. Brewster and Mrs. Merrilee never had children of their own, and Mrs. Wilbur lost two of hers to the sickness. These women – and their men – are glad enough to open their arms and wagons to those poor children, so we'll hope that means the making of good new homes.

Men help widows learn how to hitch and lead their teams themselves, and we women have our hands full teaching widowers how to make supper and look after their little ones.

It makes us all feel older to drive over each grave and leave it behind us on the trail. But we still want to make it to Oregon. Maybe it makes us even more stubborn. Now we're doing it not only for ourselves but also for those who have died trying to do it. It's all we can do for them now, and we're determined we will.

June 4 –

Day before yesterday, we went over a hill, then came to a place called Ash Hollow. I

Home on the Trail

guess the hill wasn't much compared to the mountains we'll have to wrestle with later, but it looked big enough to me. Ash Hollow is named right enough – there were lots of ash trees there, and the whole place is rounded out of the land, like a bowl, or maybe the hollow of a big hand. God's hand? Well, whatever it was, we were grateful for it.

No one has gotten sick in the last two days, nor have we had any more die. One of the single men, Mr. Vining, is still abed in his wagon, but he looks better today, so maybe our cholera is at an end.

There's no better place to take a deep breath and rest a spell from our troubles than here. Such a nice place to camp! It's cool and shady under the trees. There's good fresh spring water for our thirsty mouths and barrels and a chance to ease our tired bones. People put their tiredness aside and had an easier feeling in camp that night, speaking more than just the necessaries to each other, with a few welcome smiles and even a bit of laughter. It was good to hear it.

We had the Markers "in for supper" as we called it, as if we were at home and could set a nice table (which we couldn't here, of course). I cooked up beans for a change, putting dried pumpkin in with them, and Susannah hauled out some dried apple rings and made her special kind of fried apples for us. Marcus and Ethan got out their pipes and talked about farming while the stars came out, and Susannah and I put the children (who were tired after some rowdy tree-climbing) to bed. Then we had our own hen session over another cup of coffee.

Ash Hollow was a breath of fresh air for all of us, or maybe that was just the breeze through the trees. We were sorry to leave the next morning, but we put our shoulders to the yoke again manfully, with a will – or in some cases, womanfully.

June 9 –

Cyrus had told us we'd see some strange sights along the trail, and today we did – a huge mountain of solid rock coming straight up from the flat land around it and looking for all the world like a courthouse, which is what Cyrus says people call it: Courthouse Rock. Then there's Jail Rock close by, for what would a courthouse be without a place to put the bad folks?

This land is so different from Michigan! There aren't many trees, except a few clumped along the river, or around something like this Courthouse Rock. Even so, they're not big trees like back home. It's so flat

Home on the Trail

here, you can see almost forever – over the tall prairie grass to the edge of the sky. It's hard to believe Oregon is even farther than that.

June 10 –

We hadn't traveled far beyond Courthouse Rock before we saw another strange sight called Chimney Rock, a tall stick of rock that went up high into the air, like a house chimney or a church steeple. If I'd gotten here first, I would have called it Steeple Rock. But it could be that the fellow who named it wasn't exactly the churchgoing kind. It's such an oddity – a rock spire reaching out of the middle of this flat land up toward the clouds, like a finger pointing to heaven.

When you see something like this, it makes you want to stop a while and look, or make camp, even if it's not time yet. But there's always the need to keep moving, to keep putting miles on the behind side of you. So after a few of us have stopped for a bit as an excuse to rest or tighten up our wagons again, Cyrus will round us up and push us back on our way.

He says we need to get to a place called Independence Rock around the beginning of July, and we'll have quite some traveling to do in order to make it. Now that's a place I couldn't picture right off from the name of it, but Cyrus says it's because you need to get there by Independence Day, that being July Fourth. It's sort of a marking point, so your train can make certain it's doing all right. I hope we are.

When we were leaving the town of Independence, that jumping-off place way back, it seemed our wagon train was so big and important, like a whole town that would be moving across the land. Now, out on the prairie where there's so much space, it seems like the whole train together is pretty small, not at all what you'd call important-looking. It's kind of like a line of ants plunked down in the middle of a pie plate.

June 12 –

Saw our first Indians today! All of a sudden, there they were on their horses, off to the north. Startled us some, so we stopped the wagons. As the Indians rode in close, our men took up a party of Cyrus, Marcus and some others to see what they wanted. We all hoped it wasn't our scalps. There were a few worrisome moments, I can tell you, when we saw those Indians come near, looking real stern, like a schoolteacher or preacher does when he's trying to make you behave.

Home on the Trail

The men parleyed a little and decided it would be a good thing if we gave them something, so they took up a collection and came up with some cornmeal and a length of calico. That seemed to break the ice a bit.

A couple of us women thought if we weren't going to die real soon, it might be neighborly to offer coffee, so we started up a fire and put some on to boil. Then, as sudden as those Indian men appeared before, here came their women out of nowhere. Heavens, they're quiet on how they move about! Clara McCreedy pushed the idea that this was probably so their men could murder our men while their women did us in, all according to the Indian rule of doing things. But it didn't seem a likely thought, if only because it was Clara who had it. Besides, the coffee was done, so we went ahead with our plan and offered it to them all. We had a reasonable time of it, considering we were different, and couldn't talk to each other much. Wasn't like after Sunday meeting, but then this is the trail, after all.

After the coffee, the Indian women brought out some of what they call moccasins. The Indians make and wear this kind of shoe themselves, and I must say, they were what you'd call a real workmanlike job. I traded a small bag of coffee for some, and it was a fair exchange. Having looked real careful at the Indians' feet before I did my trading, I saw those moccasins seem to hold up well, even with a lot of walking. So all our family got new shoes, and the Indians got some coffee for more socializing like we showed them how to do.

Different people don't seem so different somehow, once you meet up with them face to face. At least that's what I thought, and was proud to have met my first Indians. Clara said our trading was just a scandal, and she thought we ought to shut all the children up in the wagons with sheets over them, as if the children getting hot and stuffy under sheets would keep them safe from Indian arrows and tomahawks. She didn't share in the coffee hour, but went around gasping like a fish, rolling her eyes, and saying she expected to be murdered any minute.

Mrs. Wickham told me privately that maybe it wouldn't have been so bad if the Indians had used Clara's idea of the murdering – but only for Clara. I told her that was unkind to say. But I waited just a minute to let us both think before I said it.

June 13 –

Passed by Scott's Bluff today. The place is

called that since there was a trader by the name of Scott who died here. Our train had to narrow up and go one after the other for a change, to get through a skinny place in the rocks. The bluff is so high, if you were standing on the top, I bet you could see all the way to Oregon City. Makes it seem not quite so far off. But it is, I know, and there's more walking than I want to think about before we get there.

Put on our Indian moccasins today and they're real comfortable. Matt about wore himself out running around and giving his idea of Indian war whoops. He'd come up behind me and whoop, and I'd act real scared. But to tell the truth, it was more of a job not to laugh, as his little whoop is closer to a happy squeal than a bloodthirsty warning.

When we stopped for lunch, Hester and I talked about some of the sights we've seen lately, and she took a stick and drew Chimney Rock in the dirt to see if she could remember it right. A real good likeness, I thought. Maybe being on the trail is like schooling to the children, they'll learn so much.

June 16 –

The other day, a foolish thing happened. Lawrence Simpson shot himself in the leg. With as much as these men handle their guns, you'd think they'd learn to be more careful. I didn't ask too deeply into the details of how it happened. He was probably loading or cleaning it, I'd guess, but careless, no doubt, and I'm not about to feel sorry the way I normally do when an innocent person gets hurt.

Lawrence's wife was scared he'd lose his leg over it. But Mrs. Bates, with her large family of menfolk and her midwifery, is familiar with these matters, and she got busy and cleaned the wound up real good so it wouldn't fester. The bullet had gone straight through, so she didn't have to do any digging around inside for it, which was just as well for Lawrence, as white-faced as he looked after the cleaning-up.

For some reason, Lacey Cogburn got it in her head that Nathan Wickham had been in considerable danger from all this, since he was only about a quarter of a mile away when Lawrence shot himself. And since Nathan's only a big strapping boy who can lift a fifty-pound sack of flour like it's a teacup, Lacey had no doubt he was disturbed enough by the whole matter to need some serious comforting. So she went to him and comforted something fierce, with sweet words and a good deal of laying her hand on his arm. And while it seemed unlikely Nathan had been afraid, he didn't look like he found the comforting unwelcome.

Meanwhile, his ma, Mrs. Wickham, had more of an eye to the whole train's benefit (knowing her son could take care of himself, except maybe around Lacey), and took it upon herself to go to Cyrus and have a no-nonsense talk. She told him the men ought to be more careful, otherwise we'd wind up with a dead child or woman, or someone other than the gun-toter – someone who did not deserve it. Well, having seen Mrs. Wickham when she gets her dander up about something, I can just about guess what she told Cyrus, and how she said it.

He looked like he wished he could say what did a woman know about it anyway, and why was she putting him in the middle? But he didn't realize just how lucky he was that he only had to listen to Mrs. Wickham representing all the women. He'd have been worse off if each of us had set upon him and had our say individually, since we mostly felt the same – and pretty firmly about it, too.

So Cyrus had his talk with the men that night. When Marcus came back to the wagon afterward, I pried it loose from him that what Cyrus said was if they didn't be careful with their guns, they'd wind up with a whole bunch of women down their backs about it –

which would be worse than a gunshot wound in the long run. Wise man, that Cyrus.

June 18 –

Went across the Laramie River yesterday, the first river we've had to cross in weeks. I wondered if we'd forget how to do it, but we didn't. These traveling ways stay with you once you learn them. Now this may sound like a fool's errand, but here's how it worked: We were going along beside the Platte, but the Laramie came right in front of us and cut us off, since it spills out into the Platte on the same side where we were traveling. So we had to go over the Laramie to keep on our way alongside the Platte! I tell you, it seems as if nothing stops us anymore – we just keep rolling those wagon wheels westward.

Then we got to Fort Laramie, and Cyrus said we're now a third of the way to Oregon City. Only a third of the way! It feels like we've been traveling forever! I can hardly remember how cold it was when we started out, how we used to huddle up in the wagon with our clothes on underneath all the blankets every night and still get cold.

Fort Laramie is one of those stocked with Army soldiers to protect folks going through

Home on the Trail

on the trail, in case Indians decide to attack. It appears that Indian people everywhere aren't as friendly as the ones we happened to run into, especially the more westerly you go. They don't like people crossing through the land they say is theirs.

Now how can the land belong to the Indians, if it's the government's, too?

But then, the government had to build these forts pretty recently, and the Indian people were already here, so I don't know. Things are always more confused in life than you think when you first look at them. Seems the older I get, the more confused I get. Maybe people don't really die at all, they just get too muddled to continue.

We had ourselves a fort day here as usual, stocking up on fresh water and supplies, resting, doing laundry, children raising Cain and things like that. I wrote more letters to the folks back home, spilling my heart to my ma and Mary Ann about the cholera sickness and all we've seen. And I wrote that I was thinking about the good things that should be coming up now in Eleanor's garden from the seeds I left her: radishes, lettuce, peas, tomato plants still looking a little thin maybe and cucumbers for pickles reaching their viny fingers up the fence. My mouth started watering so bad for a nice crisp radish that I had to fin-

Mona Exinger

ish up those letters right quick and trot off to leave them with the Army men to send back East.

From here on, we're done with the flat prairie and will be heading toward those big mountains. You can see it already in the way the land is changing. Before, there was tall grass on the plains with a few trees along the rivers, but here there aren't any trees at all, the grass is skimpier, and mixed in with it are little scrubby bushes called sagebrush. They give off a kind of sharp sagey smell when you crumple the leaves in your fingers. I like it, although some of the women say it stinks. And there are lots of other kinds of plants and flowers that we've never seen before.

Hester likes to explore and get out in the grass to see what she can, and I don't blame her. It's interesting to see new things, and it takes some of the boredom out of walking all day. But I tell her over and over to be careful and not go off too far, as the memory of little Jake Huggins getting bit by that rattler still hangs heavy with me. While Marcus walks along with the team and wagon, keeping an eye on Matt, sometimes I walk out in the grass right along with Hester, to keep her company and see more myself.

I'm not looking forward to the mountains. Cyrus says we've never seen anything like

Home on the Trail

them, and that's why people were warned against loading their wagons too heavily.

June 19 –

After we left Fort Laramie today, we passed a place where another trail met up with ours. Susannah and I were walking along together, and she happened to look back and see what might have been wagons behind us and off to the side. It's hard to describe what a wagon far off on the trail looks like – dust and something moving, is all. What draws your eye is the movement, a piece that doesn't quite belong in the normal stillness of the land.

Well, it gave us quite a start. Then she and I rattled on to each other about what would happen when these folks – if what we'd seen were wagons – caught up and joined us. We'd have a bigger camp at night, and it would be nice to have different people to talk to. It's not exactly that we're so deadly tired of everyone in our train (not so we'd admit it to each other, anyway), but it sounded good to have a chance at some fresh faces and conversation. Guess it wasn't to be, though – no sooner were we getting interested in meeting them, than we looked back and it seemed they were dropping out of sight.

After a while, we wondered if we were

going trail-crazy and hadn't really seen anything at all. Things like that happen, you know. Folks get so tired of traveling they start seeing things that aren't there, but I never thought that would happen to two sensible gals like Susannah and me. We decided not to mention it to anyone else, lest we sound odd. So we kept to ourselves and walked along quietly, trying to see in other people's faces when they looked at us, whether it was too late, and we looked trail-crazy already.

When we camped tonight, curiosity got the better of me, and I went to ask Cyrus what it was we might have seen. He said it was people who've been on a different trail north of us until now, and from here on we'll all be traveling the same path. We couldn't stop to let them catch up, since we need to get to Independence Rock soon, and there's still a long way to go.

I was relieved not to have been trail-crazy, after all. At least, not yet.

June 20 –

Today we saw Register Cliff. It was a big rock face where people carve their names, the date, or maybe even a message to others coming along behind them on the trail. We stopped for lunch and ate quickly, so we'd

Home on the Trail

have time to read some of the writings on the rock before we had to move on. No matter on the lunch – we could skip meals now if we didn't get so hungry – since the food's only what we're already tired of, anyway. But having a chance to give your mind over to something fresh, like these writings, perked up everybody.

Marcus spent his time carving "Patience" on the rock as an inspiration to other tired travelers, and I was glad he thought of it. The children and I read names and messages and tried to remember as much as we could to tell him later at supper.

My, it was interesting to read all that! And of course we read out loud, so those who couldn't read wouldn't feel bad or miss anything. You come to know who can't read – and there's quite a number – because they tend to hang back like they feel ashamed and don't want other folks to notice. It's not their fault, though. Perhaps there wasn't a school nearby when they were children, or they couldn't be spared from the farm to go. The thing to do is read out loud and clear and include people by looking right at them and saying something like, "Charles Bowen. Says he was here last year. Do you suppose, Margaret, that he's any relation to that Bowen fellow you told me of who lived over your way at home?"

Mona Exinger

That sassy little Lacey dragged Nathan over to carve something on the cliff for her. I noticed it took a lot of time and giggling to accomplish a few scrapes in the rock. Wasn't too long before Mr. Cogburn roared her name so the world could hear, and Lacey scooted off back to her wagon. No, come to think of it, what she did was really too slow to call scooting – it was pretty reluctant, with a lot of turning back to smile and wave at Nathan.

We get so bored, already knowing for weeks past all we could possibly tell each other about ourselves, that it was good to talk and wonder about the Register Cliff writings. Keeping Hester and Matt distracted and making up stories to tell them gets harder all the time.

Poor children! It must feel like they've been walking forever, as if they've always had a home on wheels and only ever eaten biscuits and salt pork. Sometimes when I see one of them's getting too tired, I'll have Marcus stop the wagon, so I can put the poor child to bed for a while. Matt'll fight it, but he'll be asleep in a minute. Hester gets restless, because she can't see where we're going, all buried amongst barrels, sacks and blankets. So after a while, it's enough of that, and she's got to pop out and start walking again. Too much of me in her, I guess – can't stand to miss a thing.

Home on the Trail

June 25 –

I could hardly believe it, but today we crossed the Platte River for the very last time! It's been our companion for so many weeks, I almost feel bad about leaving it, except it shows we're that much farther along.

Now it's time to put aside the familiar and find a new way, and that's what the trail is all about – reaching out and grasping new things. I remember when the Platte itself was new and strange to us, but now we'll have other rivers to cross and mountains to climb over. Frankly, I haven't been looking forward to these mountains – they sound like so much work. But I'll try to remember and take my own advice about reaching out for the new. You can tell the land is getting ready to make mountains, too. It rolls away in broad swells as far as you can see.

We heard tell of plans to build a bridge at this place over the Platte, but there's only a ferry here now. It's run by some of those Mormon folks, who always seem to be a busy group. Everybody's busy out here in the West, I suppose, with so much work to do making sense of the wilderness.

A bridge would surely be an improvement. Maybe if we'd waited more years before coming out, all the rivers would have had bridges.

Mona Exinger

But then maybe the best land in Oregon would be taken, too. You have to do what seems right at the time, and I believe it was our time to come now, even if things are rough and raw. I like being in on beginnings, to help out where it's needed.

June 26 –

After going over the Platte, we camped at Fort Caspar, the last fort we'll see for quite a while, and made the most of it – filling up water barrels, checking supplies and wagons, doing laundry. (To be honest, the laundry was only a halfhearted, slapdash effort; we're all so dirty and our clothes in such poor shape, we just do it because we think we should, not because we're getting it that much cleaner.) We won't get to the next fort until after the mountains, so we need to make sure everything's sturdy and well-packed now. The men considered staying another day to rest the animals, but they decided against it. Everyone's in reasonable shape, considering all we've been through so far.

Cyrus told us we were ahead of where he was at this time of year when he came before. That made me feel like we'd done a good job. But so we wouldn't get swelled heads, he followed it right up by saying the sooner we get

Home on the Trail

to Oregon, the better to ready ourselves for wintering-over. We expect to arrive sometime in the fall, and I don't know exactly how we'll get through this first winter. But we did hear the winters there aren't nearly as cold and snowy as back home.

Tonight after supper, Ethan came over, and he and Marcus talked about what they'd need to do for settling in before winter. Choosing your land is the first thing, of course. Then if there's no spring on your land, you've got to dig a well before you build your cabin.

Susannah strolled over after she put Johnny to bed, and we chatted on about all we'd have to do to help our men, and more besides. There's so much work, but it's exciting, too, to think about making a home where everything'll be new and fresh and all of your very own doing.

Map

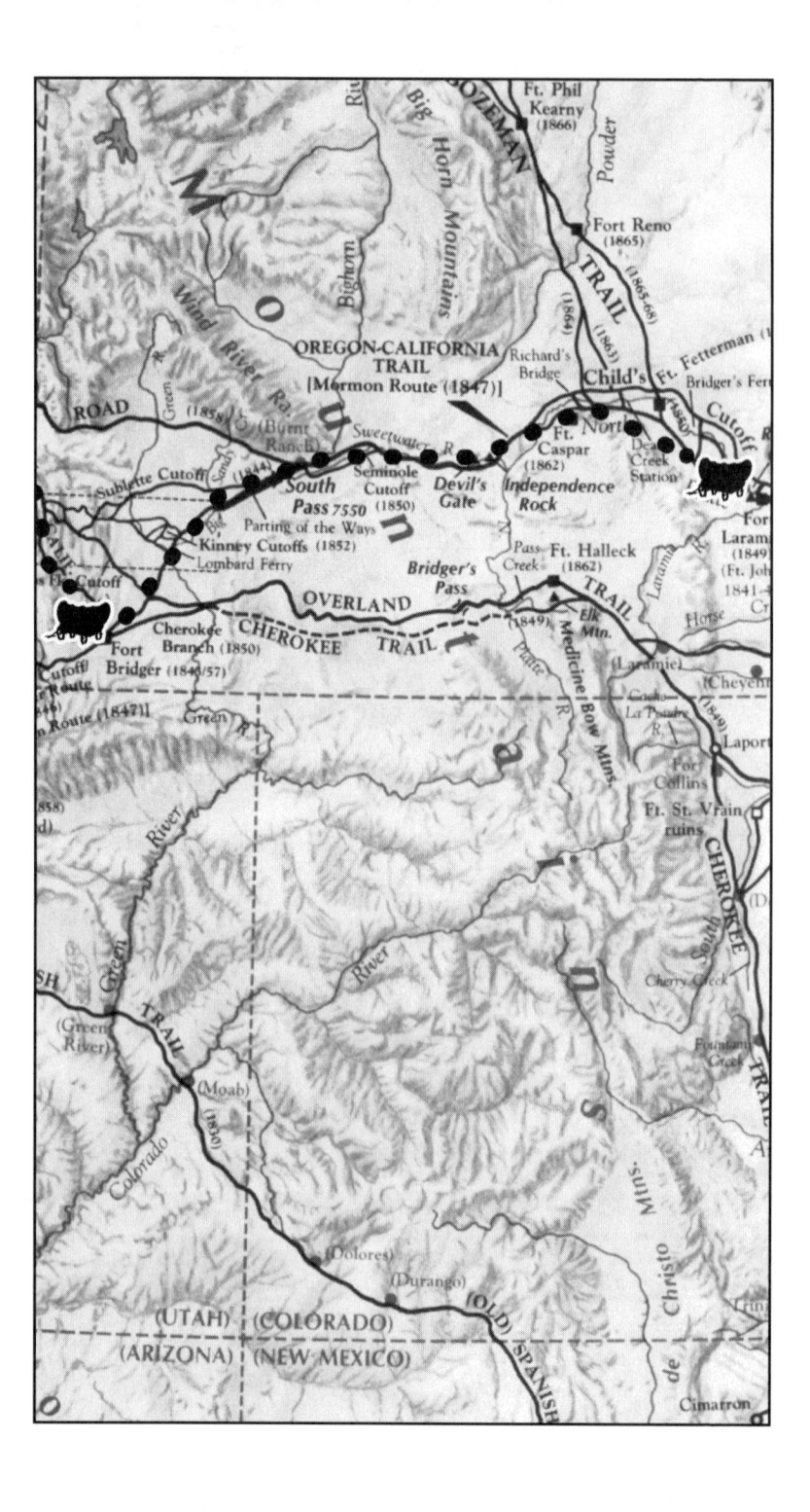

Ft. Phil Kearny (1866)
Fort Reno (1865)
BOZEMAN TRAIL (1865-68)

Big Horn Mountains
Bighorn R.
Powder R.
Wind River Range

OREGON-CALIFORNIA TRAIL [Mormon Route (1847)]

Richard's Bridge (1864)
Child's (1863)
Ft. Fetterman
Bridger's Ferry

ROAD (1858)
Green R.
Sandy
(Burnt Ranch)
Sweetwater R.
Ft. Caspar (1862)
Deer Creek Station

Sublette Cutoff (1844)
South Pass 7550
Seminole Cutoff (1850)
Devil's Gate
Independence Rock
Ft. Laramie (1849) (Ft. John 1841-)

Parting of the Ways
Kinney Cutoffs (1852)
Lombard Ferry
Pass Creek
Ft. Halleck (1862)
Laramie R.
Horse Cr.

Cutoff
Bridger's Pass
TRAIL

OVERLAND (1849)
Cherokee Branch (1850)
CHEROKEE TRAIL
Elk Mtn.
Medicine Bow Mtns.

Fort Bridger (1846/57)
(Laramie)
(Cheyenne)

Cutoff Route (1847?)
Green R.
La Poudre R.
Laport
Fort Collins
Ft. St. Vrain ruins
CHEROKEE

Green River
(Green River)
TRAIL
Cherry Creek
Fountain Creek

(Moab) (1850)
Colorado R.

(Dolores)
(Durango)
Sangre de Cristo Mtns.

(UTAH) (COLORADO) (OLD)
(ARIZONA) (NEW MEXICO) SPANISH

Cimarron

Chapter Seven

July

July 3 –

Independence Rock at last! We got here yesterday, and it was worth all the pushing along on the trail, as we were two whole days early.

We declared the Fourth of July holiday early, too, and had ourselves a celebration. The men were glad because being here so soon means we'll cross the mountains in time to beat the snow. It comes early there. They were all rousting around, joking, and feeling in a party mood. That got the children going, of course, so there was nothing left for us women to do but join in. We got our chores done as fast as we could. Then everyone scrounged around in their supplies to see

Home on the Trail

what we had fit for a party. There wasn't much, but we made what we could of it.

A row of barrels and boxes lined up had to serve as our table, but after we spread some quilts on them for a little color, then laid all the food out on top, it looked fine (though I couldn't help but think one of Mary Ann's apple pies would have come in handy). So we dug in and had ourselves a real community social.

There was even singing and dancing. It started out official and serious with a couple of hymns, and we offered a prayer of thanks for the meal and our progress on the trail. But before long, somebody broke into one of the old songs – you know, the ones that nobody even knows who thought them up, because folks've been singing the same ones since before you were born. Ethan brought out his jew's-harp and laid into it, and Marcus hauled out an empty nail keg and started beating on it like a drum. That man!

Lacey waited as long as she could before she sashayed over to ask Nathan to dance – I noticed she did it when her pa's back was turned – then another couple joined them and another. Before you knew it, we were all out there whooping it up and having a gay old time. Our singing wasn't much to listen to, but it was put forth with a good will, and the dancing was just plain fun. I grabbed Matt up and whirled him around until we were both so dizzy we couldn't see straight, and giggling to beat the band – what there was of it.

As the evening wore on, the dancing slowed down, and you'd begin to come across a small heap of a child or two snuggled on the ground asleep, worn out from celebrating. Families drifted off to their wagons to bed, and the party faded away, until finally you could hear all the little night noises of the land, familiar and comforting to us now, we've been hearing them so long.

This morning, as we packed up to leave, some of the men carved on the rocks to leave a reminder that our train was here, like we did at Register Cliff. Marcus carved our family name and the date, and it was a good, readable job. I hope when someone else passes along here, they'll see it and wonder who we are.

July 5 –

Since Independence Rock, we've been following a new river, the Sweetwater, which lives up to its name as better-tasting than any we've had for some time. At home I guess we took water for granted, never giving a thought about it. But on the trail, it's a differ-

Home on the Trail

ent situation entirely. Some of what we've had wasn't very clear and tasted nasty to boot, but water's so scarce many places, you have to take what there is.

With bad water, if you poured it into your bucket and let it set for a while, the "floaters" would settle down; then you could carefully pour the clear water off the top, trying not to stir up the bottom stuff into it. That's all right if you're in camp at night and have the time, but when you only stop for lunch and the wagon's been bumping along all morning, jostling that water up in the barrel – well, you just pour it out, drink it, and try not to look too closely.

July 10 –

Today was Matt's birthday and my little boy turned a big seven years old. Poor child, it wasn't much of a celebration for him – not like we would have had at home – but we did the best we could and got up extra early in the morning to do it.

Matt's hair was getting long, and I'd seen him swiping it away from his face lately, so my present was to give him a haircut right away when he got up. Doesn't sound like such a good gift, but he seemed pleased enough at the idea and held real still for me,

Mona Exinger

even though he was a bit sleepy yet. Afterward, he told me he was glad I thought to do it, since one of the Atkins boys has hair so long the others called him a sissy the other day and made terrible fun of him. Matt didn't want to find himself in the same situation.

After the haircutting, Marcus snatched the boy up and ran off to the river, where they both had an early morning bath, along with quite a spell of giggling. The idea as it was told to me was to get the hair off Matt so he wouldn't get itchy under his shirt that day, and I thought it was a fine opportunity for some cleanliness as well. As it turned out, there was a sight more horseplay than scrubbing that went on, but with all the splashing and ducking under, both my men came back sparkling, anyway.

At home we would have had a big family dinner with folks over and a real iced cake, but we are on the trail now and had to make do. So I made special corncakes for breakfast and stuck seven little twigs in for candles, and we lit the ends and sang the birthday song. There was a bit of a ruckus at the end when the twigs burned down faster than Matt could blow them out and they started scorching the corncakes. But we all helped him blow, and with a little slap of the dishrag, it was over in a minute with only a

Home on the Trail

couple of the cakes black on the edges.

Then Hester and Marcus gave Matt their presents. Hester was proud as she could be of hers; she'd taken a square of muslin and hemmed it for a handkerchief, then stitched "Matthew" on one corner and "7 years" on another in red thread. The words weren't all that straight, but Matt's eyes lit up that his big sister would do something so fine for him. He folded it carefully and stuck it in his pocket to stay as clean as possible and most likely never be used.

Marcus had saved a good piece of whittling wood, all the way since Ash Hollow, out of which he'd carved a little team and wagon. We all gasped when we saw it. I forget the skill Marcus has when he takes the time. Such detail! The ox team was beginning to step out, the wagon's canvas top rippling like it does in the breeze, and there were a couple of kegs fastened on the outside right where ours are. But the best part was the family. Up in the front, the pa drove the team with the ma alongside him, and around in the back, a girl sat swinging her legs, looking over at where the flap was being pulled aside by a boy peeking out.

It was a wonderful present, and we were still passing it around when the first move-forward call came. Cyrus always gives two calls, the first one as a warning a few minutes beforehand, then the second one to move out with our wagons. So we bustled around and got breakfast cleaned up and everything stowed. Matt asked me to put his carved wagon away in a safe place until lunch time, when he'd show it around to his friends.

I'd told Hester she might take a whole day off bossing her brother, and it looked like she heeded my words. As we started out, I saw the two of them catch up to a crowd of youngsters, and she announced in a proud way, and with a toss of her head, that today was Matt's birthday, and he was seven, making it sound very old and important indeed.

July 11 –

Cyrus said our way through the mountains was called South Pass, and going through it would mean we're halfway to Oregon City and the end of the trail. Halfway! I feel as though I've been walking my whole life, and it'll take the rest of my life to get there.

I'd thought the mountains would be like one pile of rocks bigger than any I'd ever seen, and that we'd climb over the whole pile at once. But it hasn't been that way at all. They're that big, for sure, but more like separate hills. Once you go up one, you have to go down it before you go up the next one.

Home on the Trail

Even the bit we've been through already was awful hard work, and there's a lot more ahead. Needless to say, we're glad not to have any more in our wagon than we do.

What's more, I could hardly tell when we were going through South Pass. I thought a pass would be a real skinny place we'd have to scoot through one at a time. But we were just traveling along, spread out in this wide valley, when Cyrus rode back with a grin big as all get out and asked how it felt to be going through the pass. I'd been looking hard for the last few days and was afraid I'd miss it. I would have, too, if he hadn't told me.

Even though we're only halfway, we *are* halfway. No turning back now, since each step makes that many more behind us and fewer in front. You could see in people's faces how much it helped to know that. It gave them new strength to go on. Seems every time we get discouraged and feel we're being tested a little too far, a word's passed around like this that perks us all up. Brings good thoughts of Oregon back to mind again while your feet are plodding along.

Boredom is our worst enemy on the trail. If you have something to think or talk about, the time passes a little easier, and you don't notice how tired your feet are – at least, not for a while.

Mona Exinger

July 15 –

Traveling's hard on all of us. Sometimes you have to find a way to let loose a little; otherwise you get cross and start snapping over nothing.

The men seem to handle it in their own way, but I go off with Susannah and laugh at something foolish, like how dirty and shabby everyone looks these days. We get to giggling about how the preacher at home would show us the door if we came to Sunday service looking like this.

Susannah says if she walked right up to her folks' house today, her ma'd chase her away with a broom and scold her for being a beggar and a ragamuffin. She wouldn't know her own daughter for the way her dress was torn and mended, like a patchwork quilt. Mine's the same. I think Mary Ann would hardly recognize me for the dirt on my face – maybe she'd think I was an Indian. I've been wishing she and Susannah could meet sometime, as I think they'd take to each other and be good friends. But I don't suppose it'll happen in this life.

The children try hard, but they have more arguments than at home. They get vexed from too much walking and not enough play, and never hope of any sweets, even for best behavior. Children grow up faster on the trail, that's for sure.

Home on the Trail

I think this traveling makes people tougher, with all we've had to go through, and by the time we get to Oregon – if we ever do – the ones who make it will be the kind of good sturdy folks you need in a new place like that.

July 18 –

Two days ago, it stormed just before we got to the Green River, and the water was too rough for the ferry to take us across. So we camped and waited in an awful, drizzly rain. The few rainy days we've had haven't been much to sneeze at – not hard, and not all day, like in Michigan. We usually keep right on moving in it. But this time we couldn't do anything except wait. The waiting and the drizzling didn't improve anyone's temper, and we wasted a whole day. It was the men who were the crossest, cooped up in their wagons with nothing to do but grumble about the miles we weren't making. For myself, I was glad for a day's rest.

I always try to keep ahead with my bread and biscuit-making, in case we get stuck like this and can't make a fire. We had cold meals of leftover biscuits and dried apples. Everybody ate off napkins in their laps, and we pretended it was a picnic – no need for our tin plates, since I couldn't fry our salt pork or cook any beans.

We put a good face on the day, and it passed easily enough.

There was still work to do, mind you: I had to catch up on mending our holey, patchwork clothes. It's terrible how hard all this traveling is on everything! I don't think any of Matt's shirts have the same buttons he left home with, or that match each other. Most are off in the bushes on the prairie somewhere, keeping the crows company. While I was mending, Hester was good enough to read to me – a story about pirates and also one from the Bible. Both were quite enjoyable and to my taste.

Fortunately for us women – since our husbands' tempers were not of a heat we wanted to put up with for another whole day in the wagons – the next day was clear enough, even though the river was moving along pretty quickly.

The ferryman was a grouchy sort, and it's my opinion he turned to his advantage the odd chance that it had rained right before we arrived. He bellyached about how the rain wasn't his fault, the water was awful fast, he didn't want to take a chance on losing his raft, and on and on. Take a chance! What did he think we were doing? Here we were, with everything we owned in these wagons, needing to get ourselves across the river and willing to trust

Home on the Trail

him to do it, and all he could do was fuss.

Finally he allowed as how he'd take us over, but it would cost an extra two dollars for each wagon – "for the extra trouble," as he said. Well, that riled my temper up in turn, and I told Marcus if the man was going to charge us for the extra trouble anyway, I'd be certain to make some for him, so we'd at least get our money's worth. He shushed me to not make the situation worse and said he was glad enough just to be moving on the way again.

We paid our two dollars extra, and the ferrying across was rough. It would have made me nervous if I hadn't been mad already. Usually I can only feel strongly one way at a time, and since my feelings were already busy being angry, there was no room left over for nervousness.

July 20 –

Everyone's so tired all the time, and little things people do for each other can mean a lot. Folks hardly have any extra gumption left in them, so if they manage to scrape up a bit to do for someone else, it's seen as a real gift and a kindness.

If you see a woman who's got it all sapped out of her, you take her baby to carry up a hill for her. If you notice in camp that somebody's a bit shy with their supper fixings because their supplies are getting low, you sidle on up to them with a little bag of flour or coffee you've been holding back. Then you say, "Rachel, I just repacked my wagon, and I can't find a place for this flour now with everything rearranged. Hester wants that spot for her doll to sleep, and you know there's no use arguing with a tired child. By any chance, could you take it off my hands? I'd be obliged to you, as I can't bear to waste it."

Doing it real casually is the important part. People feel bad enough about being poor and worn out, without worrying about the fact that you know it, too. Not that our family has much extra left now, but we ought to share what we have. And with all of us at our wits' end, if not the trail's end yet, what you see in people's eyes when you do something for them is all the thanks you might need.

July 23 –

For days, we've been looking ahead to Fort Bridger. It's been so long since we had a chance at a fort day for resting and laundry and maybe some new supplies. Now that we've gotten here, it's almost nothing – small and shabby, and not even any Army. It was just started by some man named Bridger as his trading post.

Home on the Trail

Even so, we hauled in and stopped for a day, as some had need of the blacksmith.

I'd written some letters, and I left them here, but wondered if they'd even make it out of this poor place to the folks back East. Kept my writing short and tried not to sound too lonely or discouraged. But even so, I had to wipe a few tears off the one to Mary Ann. Hope she doesn't notice.

We happened to meet some Mormon folks at the fort; a lot of them travel along the trail, too. I spoke with a woman while we both did our laundry, and she sang high praises of a place called Salt Lake. She told me it was the land of milk and honey (all through here looks pretty dry to me, though). She said we ought to give up our ways, change our church and go with them.

I was polite enough, I hope, in listening to her talk, but told myself privately I could never see things her way. Sometimes Mormon men marry more than one wife, and I really couldn't do that to Marcus. That poor man has more than he can handle with just me.

July 30 –

We left the Sweetwater River some ways back, and now there's more and more dryness in the land, so we guard our water carefully. Seems most of the water in the whole country must be situated back East, with hardly any left over for out here.

This morning, Clara McCreedy made a scene before we broke camp – marched right up to Cyrus and announced she wasn't going any farther without more water. She yelled out pretty lusty, saying she wasn't a well woman to be forced on in such a manner, and it was a poor leader indeed who'd drag people into such land as this and not care a flip.

If there's one thing that woman's good at – this being the only one, from what I've seen – it's lining up angry words and firing them off at someone. She ruckused enough to rile up half a dozen other folks, too, and they all faced off against Cyrus. That little knot of people was moving in and getting angrier by the minute. I looked around to make sure no one had a gun and hoped the situation wouldn't get any uglier through Clara's start of such wickedness.

Cyrus just stood and gazed real thoughtful at Clara and her crew for a moment, then he allowed as how it was pretty dry, and he wouldn't lie to her, we'd have more of the same or even worse ahead in some spots. He said with her feeling the way she did, he couldn't force her to go on. But she might remember that if we kept moving, we'd even-

Home on the Trail

tually come upon more water, which, if she stayed put, she'd never have the benefit of, since none of us would be coming back this way to bring her any.

Everybody saw the sense of this, including some of Clara's posse, and I noticed some of them start to mumble and move away toward their wagons. But Clara isn't easily put aside, and she looked as if she was about to fire off her other barrel. Suddenly Harve Drucker pipes up, saying he'll be glad to send Clara a letter from Oregon City, but to be sure she'll have time to read his regards before she keels over from thirst, she'd best excuse him so he can be quickly on his way.

Well, that broke the crowd up into a chuckle all around and sent us to our wagons to get started and away from Clara's wrath. Everyone headed out. While I've no doubt she simmered and stewed and had wicked thoughts of all of us, I noticed later in the day the McCreedy wagon was still present amongst us and hadn't made the choice to wait for a water delivery. Clara stomped along beside it with a stormy face, but Mr. McCreedy leading his ox team made a peaceful threesome. That poor, long-suffering man.

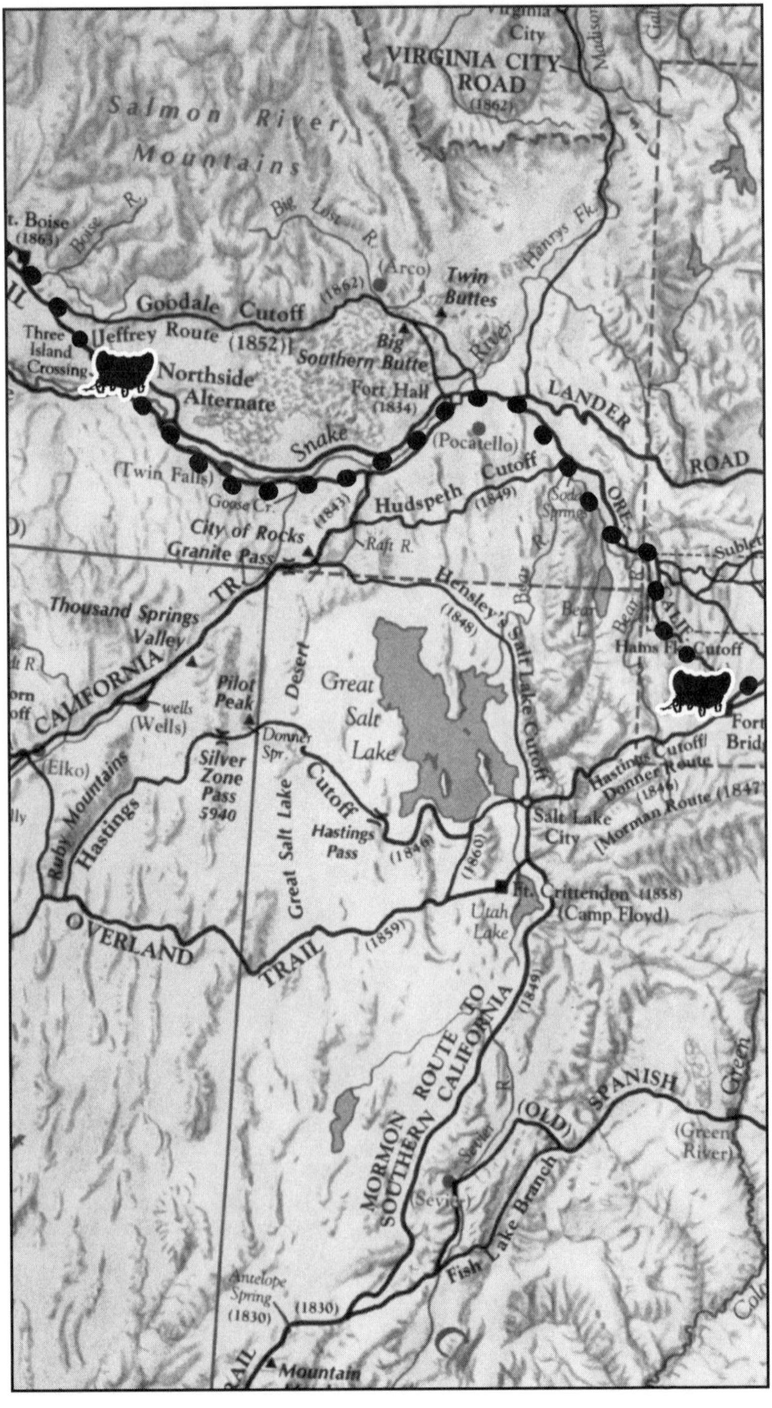
VIRGINIA CITY ROAD
(1862)
Salmon River Mountains
Big Lost R.
Boise R.
Henrys Fk.
Goodale Cutoff
(1862)
(Arco)
Twin Buttes
Jeffrey Route (1852)
Three Island Crossing
Northside Alternate
Big Southern Butte
Fort Hall (1834)
LANDER ROAD
Snake
(Pocatello)
(Twin Falls)
Goose Cr.
Hudspeth Cutoff (1849)
(1843)
City of Rocks
Granite Pass
Raft R.
Hensley's Salt Lake Cutoff (1848)
Bear R.
Bear L.
ORE.
CALIF.
Hams Fk. Cutoff
Thousand Springs Valley
CALIFORNIA TR
Pilot Peak
Desert
Great Salt Lake
wells
(Wells)
Donner Spr.
Silver Zone Pass 5940
Cutoff
Hastings Pass
(1846)
(Elko)
Ruby Mountains
Hastings
Great Salt Lake
Salt Lake City
Hastings Cutoff/ Donner Route (1846)
[Morman Route (1847
(1860)
Ft. Crittendon (1858)
(Camp Floyd)
Utah Lake
OVERLAND TRAIL
(1859)
MORMON ROUTE TO SOUTHERN CALIFORNIA
(1849)
Sevier R.
(Sevier)
(OLD) SPANISH
Fish Lake Branch
Green
(Green River)
Antelope Spring (1830)
(1830)
Mountain

Chapter Eight

August

August 3 –

For the past few days, we've been busy getting everybody up Big Hill. Certainly took no schooling and no gifted tongue to come up with a simple name like that. I would have tried a lot harder to think of something prettier or more romantic, like Lofty Climb or Heaven's Footstool. Big Hill, indeed.

Well, going over Big Hill was the same as climbing any other hill or mountain – a lot of work.

We gathered all the wagons together at the bottom and unhitched teams from some to double-hitch them to others for better pulling. Then the double-hitched wagons

Home on the Trail

went up the hill, one at a time. At the top, the teams were unhitched and brought down again to take up another wagon. Each team had to take up two wagons, one after the other, so you can see the animals had the worst share of the work. They badly needed a rest when it was over. Bob and Bert were glad to get out of their harness, and Marcus was tuckered out enough to fall asleep sitting up at dinner tonight. So I tucked him into bed early with the children.

All the people walked up the hill, of course, except old Mrs. Drucker, Nancy's mother-in-law, who rode in their wagon. She's been poorly lately, and we aren't sure she's going to make it to Oregon. Women carried babies, and Frances Prickett carried her great-grandmother's china teapot that's so dear to her. Her great-granny brought it all the way from England when she came to this country as a young girl.

Franny didn't say so, but I know she carried it in case something happened to their wagon, and it tipped or rolled back. She's babied that teapot the whole way – over rivers we've crossed and any rough land, she always held it in her arms to guard it. She's determined to get it to Oregon in one piece. I don't really think it's the pot itself, but more the remembrance and history of her family that Franny wants to

Mona Exinger

keep a piece of, way out where we're going.

It'll be something to save and give to her children later – a tie to where her people came from and how far they've traveled since.

Well, when you go up a hill, sooner or later you have to come down. It's nearly as tiring as going up and even more dangerous.

One way to do it is to cut down a small tree and tie it on the back of the wagon so it drags and slows the wagon down. Or you can cut the branches off the tree to make a pole, then put it through the back wheel spokes to lock them, so only the front two wheels can roll – and two's plenty when you're going down.

You have to use green wood for your pole so it doesn't break. Finding some along the trail is quite a trick, since there's hardly any trees at all around here.

When you see the next hill coming up, that's a good time to start looking around for something to cut and carry along with you. Women or older boys'll drag their pole up the hill so it's not extra weight on the wagon, then there it is at the top when it's needed.

Sometimes, at really bad places, you have to use the spoke-pole and have men pulling, or teams tied to the rear of the wagon to hold it back even more. This is serious business. If a wagon slips and gets away down the hill, people and animals could be killed.

Home on the Trail

Our men get pretty grumpy going up and down hills, with all the work, but they have their teamwork down pat and do it carefully. We women can't ask for cheerfulness above and beyond that – wouldn't get it, anyway.

There's mostly just a lot of work on the trail, even more than at home, and sometimes I think it's a shame Adam and Eve didn't forbear a little more from eating that apple. Then the rest of us folks could still be in the Garden of Eden and wouldn't have to work. Except that what they gained was knowledge, which is a good thing, of course.

I wouldn't want to be an empty-headed fool sitting around in that garden all my life and never know or do anything, even if it is hard work. So I guess we're better off the way things turned out.

I told Mrs. Wickham what I thought about that. She's a woman who knows her Bible – not in a fist-shaking, holding-forth kind of way, just a sensible one. She said it was an interesting opinion, and one she hadn't heard before. She was inclined to agree.

August 6 –

Yesterday, we stopped to camp at a place called Soda Springs. I'm familiar with springs of water that come up out of the ground, but

Mona Exinger

this kind was another one of those things we've come across on the trail that makes me know I haven't seen it all yet. This water tasted all poppity and bubbly in your mouth, like fireworks.

Harve Drucker comes from a bigger town than we do back East, and he said some places sell soda like this to drink, but it's flavored. Must be kind of like hard cider or beer. Not that I'd know anything about beer – well, maybe just a little.

Harve teased Clara McCreedy, saying since she was still tagging along with us for water's sake, she might as well fill her barrels up with this stuff.

I don't know about whole barrels, but some folks liked it so much, they filled up a little keg to take along with them. It really wasn't to my taste, though, and I can't imagine something like that ever catching on enough so people'd pay for it, either.

August 10 –

Arrived at Fort Hall today. No Army here, it's just a place for trading – but even so, it's nicer than Fort Bridger, the other trading fort we visited. Seems an outfit called the Hudson's Bay Company runs this one and also the next one we'll stop at, Fort Boise.

Home on the Trail

I don't know where Hudson's Bay is, there's no bays – hardly any water at all – around here, but these people seem pretty organized, like it's their business to run forts. With what most of these places charge for supplies, I suppose the way to make even more money than running one fort is to run lots of them.

August 12 –

After leaving Fort Hall, we've been traveling alongside the Snake River. It'll be our companion for quite a while. It's lovely to look at, with trees lining the banks and the water chuckling along so briskly. It's more like my view of what a river should be, instead of a bunch of shallow mud holes, like the Platte.

But Cyrus has been looking serious and watchful since we left the fort.

We have to be especially watchful here against Indian attacks. What makes the river banks pretty are the ups and downs and rock areas, but those same things make it dangerous, too – there's lots of places for Indians to hide and wait to surprise somebody on the trail. It would be awful to have worked and walked and come this far and not make it to Oregon City because you got killed by Indians here. If Indians have to kill you, they should do it way back right after Independence, so then you wouldn't have to struggle to get across the rivers and mountains, and wind up so tired right before you die.

And it's hard to think about those nice Indians we traded with as ever being mean and killing folks, but it's easy enough to see there must be bad and good Indians both, just the same as there's Clara McCreedy and me. Is that too prideful?

August 13 –

You would have thought that with everybody at their wits' end, getting so tired of traveling and wishing every day we were already in Oregon that Nathan and Lacey could have held off a bit longer. But Susannah says young love won't be held back, and I guess she's right.

Last night, before the grown-ups got settled down for the night and the first watch put on, we heard a terrible ruckus: men yelling, a girl's scream, and a gunshot or two. My hair raised up on my head for what I hoped wasn't the last time, as I feared it was Indians attacking. Marcus went for his rifle, and I grabbed up the frying pan I'd just washed. Any weapon was better than none, and I figured if there were

Home on the Trail

unfriendly Indians to be had, I'd make sure to bash a few of their skulls and protect my children as long as I could.

It only took two blinks of an eye for Marcus and I to snatch up our arms, but during those blinks, the noise settled down to what sounded like a serious cuss-fest being put forth by Mr. Cogburn, Lacey's pa. And we could see over by the fire near the Wickhams' wagon a gaggle of people was forming. The children had roused and were peeking out the wagon canvas. But I told them to go back to sleep and hoped they hadn't already learned some new words from the Cogburn storehouse.

Marcus gave me a nod to let loose the frying pan, and after he stowed his rifle safely, we headed over to the crowd to see what was up. More and more folks clustered in, and the ones on the inside who'd heard the story were turning away, men chuckling and women shaking their heads. This made me mighty curious as to how something that started so nasty could be funny in the end.

In the middle of the circle of people, right by the fire, Mr. Cogburn was waving his arms and haranguing Cyrus, who was trying to calm Mr. Cogburn down enough to take his gun away – if not talk some sense into him. Mrs. Wickham stood there with her arms crossed firmly and that set jaw she gets when she's made up her mind not to take guff from anybody. Nathan and Lacey were close by, him splitting his time between looking sheepish and patting her on the shoulder, while she was busy sobbing her eyes out. Mrs. Cogburn, her eyes following her husband's gun flapping through the air at the end of his arm, was trying to shush the rest of her girls and herd them back to their wagon. But none of the stair-steps were paying her any mind. They just crowded together in their nightgowns, tugging the same blanket around the four of themselves, giggling and pushing each other, determined to see what kind of trouble their big sister'd gotten herself into this time.

Amidst all the sobbing and giggling and patting and pushing and jaw-setting going on, Mr. Cogburn was laying into Cyrus about innocent folks' safety being protected, criminals who ought to hang and that Cyrus, being the leader, should see that justice was done, or he (Mr. Cogburn) would know the reason why.

This didn't clear matters up for me any, so I tipped my head over to Mrs. Wilbur and asked what the whole mess was about. She said Mr. Cogburn had caught Lacey and Nathan out in back of the Wickhams' wagon, doing things Lacey's pa apparently objected

Home on the Trail

to. But Mrs. Wilbur also said heavens, Nathan and Lacey are both good kids, how bad could it be? She'd stolen a kiss or two in her time – who hadn't? – and likely it was no worse than that, but you know how strict that Cogburn fellow is with his girls.

So much for our Indian attack. I was relieved it was nothing more than this and tended to agree with Mrs. Wilbur about the kisses, although I wished the two youngsters had shown more forethought than to get caught at it – at least in a country where we were already a little nervous.

By the time the whole shebang had settled down – about an hour and two pots of coffee later – Nathan had asked for Lacey's hand, promising to marry her as soon as we get to Oregon City, where there'll be a chance at finding a preacher. Lacey's pa put down his gun, her ma breathed a few sighs of relief, and the rest of the Cogburn girls took their blanket and their giggling off to bed. Mrs. Wickham, not surprised by any of it, only annoyed at Mr. Cogburn for the name-calling of her son (and involving the gun where it wasn't welcome nor needed), gave Lacey a hug and told her she'd be glad to have Lacey as a daughter-in-law, as long as she and Nathan both kept on their best behavior until the wedding.

Mona Exinger

As Marcus and I went back to our wagon for him to catch a few winks before his turn at watch, he put his arm around me and said he remembered how it was to be young and in love, how exciting it was and how it took your breath away, and didn't I remember, too? I told him being old and in love still took my breath away.

August 15 –

Our way along the Snake River gets prettier all the time. The land is so different from what it's like back in Michigan or along the prairie! Back at the home place there were trees all over, but out here in the West, there's mountains and grasslands and big open spaces. Sometimes you feel small and lonely in the middle of it, but being able to see almost forever in all directions is a wonder.

Cyrus had told us there would be a place called Thousand Springs around here, so we started watching for it. Maybe it's kind of silly, but the grown-ups get as bored as the children do, and if we can look forward to something on the trail, it makes the time pass easier.

There were springs, sure enough – a lot of them. I walked along with Susannah, Johnny, Hester and Matt, and we lost count of the ones we saw, so there could have been a thousand – tiny dribbles down the rock face, big waterfalls bursting out of nowhere and everything in between.

We had such a good time, the day went quickly. We forgot about whether our feet were tired and tried to forget about the Indians, too. All the men kept a sharp lookout, and since the children were busy counting the springs, they didn't wander off, and we could keep them close without nagging.

How much farther to Oregon City?

August 19 –

Lately, the days get hot as soon as the sun's up, so by noon we're a tired, sweaty bunch. We happened to stop near the McCreedys' wagon at lunch time today, and heard odd noises coming from inside – mostly moaning, with some snarling mixed in. Matt said through his biscuit it sounded like a witch wail, and Marcus said close enough. I said don't talk with your mouths full and went over for a look-see.

Mr. McCreedy told me Clara'd been laid out flat by what she called heat frustration, and he didn't know what to do. Well, I felt more sorry for him than her, so I shooed him over to eat lunch at our wagon and climbed up in theirs to take a peek at the wailer.

Truth be told, Clara was nothing more than hot and fussy. I bustled around and laid some wet cloths on her, made her drink a potful of tea, then dunked her sunbonnet in water, wrung it out, and told her she'd be better off outside her wagon, where the breeze on the bonnet would help cool her some. She moaned and complained the whole time – I didn't think even she heard me – so I finally went back to our wagon to pack up before the move-out call.

Mr. McCreedy tipped his hat to me and said he was obliged for the lunch and my care of Clara, and I told him he was welcome for both, even though I wasn't sure it was true.

Later, Marcus pointed out Clara dragging along in her wet bonnet and asked if Matt had been right. I flapped my apron at him and said if he didn't watch himself, I'd get myself some heat frustration, too.

August 22 –

On these long, hot days of walking, Susannah and I talk a lot about how it's going to be in Oregon. We promised to settle our families close by, so we can be neighbors and help each other. We can just see Ethan and Marcus building cabins and plowing fields, while we do our churning and washing and soapmak-

Home on the Trail

ing and all the things that go faster with another pair of hands. Our gardens will be full of vegetables and herbs and flowers, and we'll help each other plant and weed and put food up in the fall. Our children will go to school, there'll be church on Sundays, and we could even start a lending library.

Maybe some of these are only far-off dreams, but hanging hard onto such good thoughts gets us over a lot of miles on the trail.

August 29 –

What an awful time we've had the last two days! Came to where we had to cross the Snake River, and I finally figured out why they call it a snake – it's so ornery and wicked. The place was called Three Island Crossing, as there's three islands out in the middle of the water. The river's so wide here, the first crossing is only to the first island. You have to go on from there to the second, then the third, and finally to the far bank – really four crossings instead of one. The water was so deep and fast, it was almost like a flood, and I had some real doubts as to whether we'd make it at all.

First, we had to stop on the near side and put pitch on the wagons, then the men did their posseing up to take some of us over to

Mona Exinger

the first island. Susannah and I saw how scared some of the other women were, looking at all that rushing water. So we acted real brave to get their spirits up. We allowed as how we'd go in the first group, and some of the others could watch and see what to expect when they went. Nancy Drucker's a plucky gal, and she said she'd come with us, too.

Well, the next time a preacher asks me what charitable act I've done lately for others, this'll be the one I'll mention. I must have been the biggest fool in the lot, because I said I'd go first in our wagon. To get my own courage up, I remembered my grandmother used to say you can't be scared of what you haven't done yet, since you don't know just exactly what to be scared of. My grandmother didn't cross any three islands on a Snake River, that's all I have to say.

What an unholy ruckus! The river roaring, men and oxen yelling and splashing, the wagon tipping and nearly rolling over, and me with my heart in my throat so far up I couldn't swallow. Marcus and Nathan were on horses near the head of our team, with me holding the reins and hanging on tight. Hester and Matt were in the wagon box, not moving an inch, but doing it with the most worried eyes you ever saw.

After we got in the water, it was so loud, I

couldn't hear a thing.

Marcus was either yelling, "Hold 'em back!" or "Let 'em loose!" I never could tell which, so I just did the best I could by feel. The team was swimming and the wagon floating off the bottom almost right away, it was that deep. Of course we were getting pulled along by the river pretty far away from the place we went into the water, and I recall wondering what would happen if we missed the island. Would we be stuck in that river forever, floating along and looking at the riverbanks passing us by?

I didn't have much time to worry about that, because right then Nathan leaned from his horse and almost went under. I think I screamed, but who could've heard in all that commotion? He righted himself pretty quickly, but it seemed forever to me and most likely even longer to his ma and Lacey back on the bank.

You'd never believe anything could get any louder, but all of a sudden it did, and it sounded for all the world like mules screaming. That's a very unusual sound, if you've ever heard it, and one you're likely to remember. Well, whatever was happening was doing it right behind our wagon, so I thought it might be important to me, since I was the first in line and ought to know if God had

Mona Exinger

decided on a second flood with everybody else being washed under. I risked life and limb for a quick glance behind me.

Sure enough, it was a pair of mules stopped in the middle of the water. The men on horses at the head of the team tried to pull them along, but those mules wouldn't have any part of that, and they stayed put. Nancy Drucker, who was driving – well, not exactly, since the wagon wasn't moving – looked like she wished she could hop out and wash her hands of the whole mess, but she also saw it wouldn't be much use to anyone else if she did.

So she starting cracking her whip to beat the band and screaming worse than the mules. It might have been the whip, but my bet is it was the I'll-have-no-nonsense-from-you motherly tone in Nancy's voice. Nancy's children toe the line, as we all know. Anyway, the mules listened up like nobody's business and started moving fast.

When I tell it, it sounds like I gawked around for about a day, but it only took a minute. Since it looked like the second flood wasn't coming quite yet after all, and I had my own worries besides, I put my eyes in front once more and got back to the work at hand.

After only what seemed like two weeks or so, we made dry land under the wheels again, and it sure felt good. I got my hearing back

Home on the Trail

enough to hear Marcus say, "That's the first island, only two more to go." I gave him an evil look, but said nothing, since my jaw was still clamped together tight from the crossing. That's the way it was, two more of the same ahead of us before we could even get to the far bank. You can hardly turn back at that point, nor stay where you are, and since my jaw was already clamped for the ride, we just continued on. But now I knew what to be scared of, Granny.

When we got to the far bank, we checked the wagons to see what was wet and helped others as they came over. Luck or the pitch was with us, as our goods stayed pretty dry. We could only get half the train all the way over the first day, so when it got dark in the evening, we could see the fires of the rest of the folks on the far bank we'd come from, while they could see ours. That was a little lonely, to be without some of our people, and both sides seemed so small in the dark.

The next day was like the day before, with a new group of people finding out what to be scared about. Only after we'd all crossed, with no person or animal lost in the river, did Cyrus tell us how lucky that was. This crossing is the worst and most likely to have a child fall in, a team go wild and turn a wagon over, or some terrible thing. It may seem odd to say a thank-you prayer for something you didn't get, but that's what I offered up this time.

August 31 –

I never thought it could be this hot anywhere – well, almost anywhere. Every day is a scorcher, and the ground is so full of rocks it's hard on the animals, the wagons and our moccasins – to say nothing of our tired old feet. Folks back home thought they really plowed up a snootful of rocks when they broke new fields, but that's just pebbly compared to this.

Marcus says this must be the fire and brimstone they always tell you about in church, and here we are in the middle of it, even though he's tried to be a good person and isn't even dead yet. Doesn't seem quite respectful to say so, but I can't find much wrong with that idea myself.

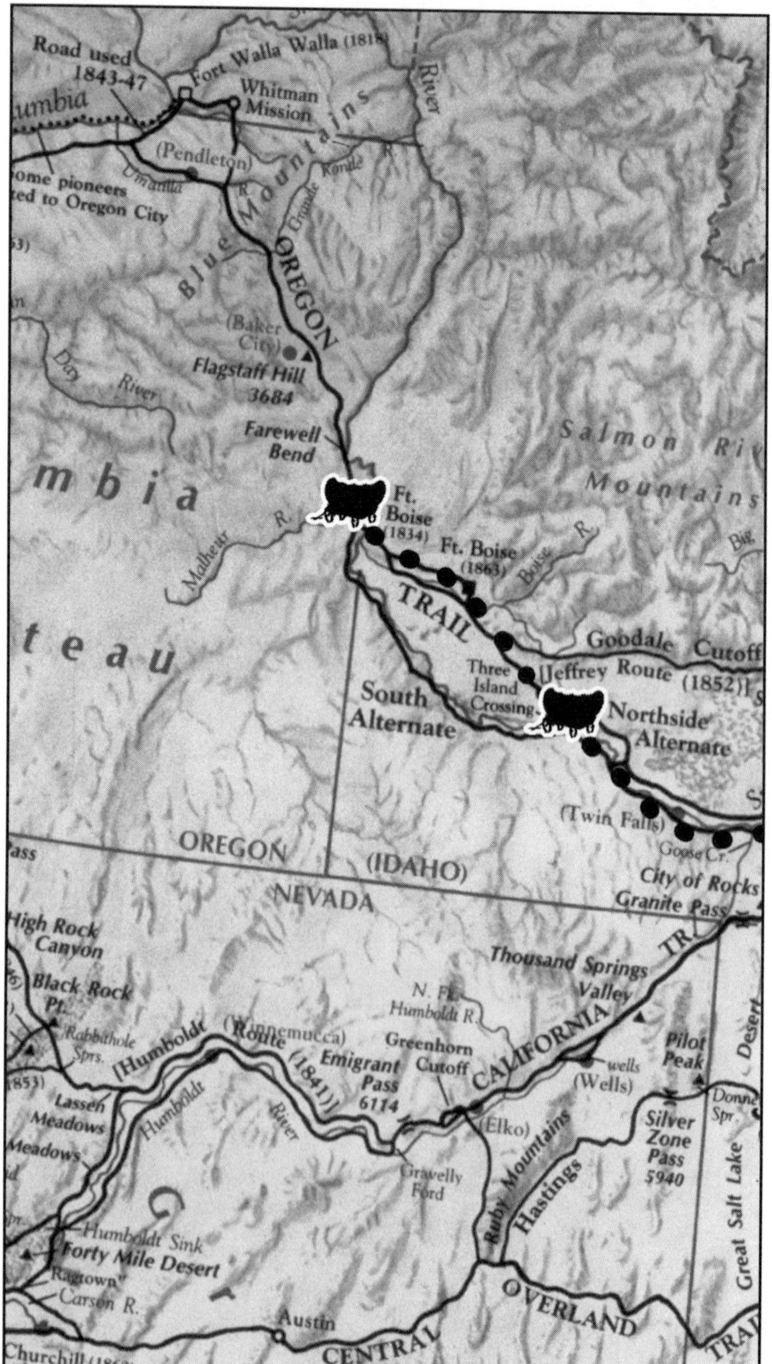

Road used 1843-47
Fort Walla Walla (1818)
Whitman Mission
(Pendleton)
Umatilla R.
Some pioneers
to Oregon City
Blue Mountains
Grande Ronde R.
River
OREGON
(Baker City)
Flagstaff Hill 3684
Day River
Farewell Bend
Ft. Boise (1834)
Ft. Boise (1863)
Malheur R.
Boise R.
Salmon River Mountains
TRAIL
Goodale Cutoff
[Jeffrey Route (1852)]
Three Island Crossing
South Alternate
Northside Alternate
(Twin Falls)
Goose Cr.
City of Rocks
Granite Pass
OREGON
(IDAHO)
NEVADA
High Rock Canyon
Black Rock Pt.
Rabbithole Sprs.
Thousand Springs Valley
N. Fk. Humboldt R.
[Humboldt Route (1841)]
(Winnemucca)
Greenhorn Cutoff
Emigrant Pass 6114
CALIFORNIA
wells
(Wells)
Pilot Peak
Lassen Meadows
Meadows
Humboldt River
(Elko)
Gravelly Ford
Ruby Mountains
Hastings
Silver Zone Pass 5940
Great Salt Lake
Desert
Humboldt Sink
Forty Mile Desert
Ragtown
Carson R.
Austin
OVERLAND
CENTRAL
Churchill (1860)

Chapter Nine

September

September 3 –

Oh, my! It's so dry everywhere the air almost crackles, and I'm so tired. I feel it must have been somebody else who started on this trip long ago in Michigan. She was a younger woman, who wasn't hot and dirty and tired and cross and thirsty all the time. Her husband wasn't so thin, and her children not so shabby-looking. The past few days I've been so thirsty, and the children have, too – they fuss at me almost to distraction. Marcus says nothing, but I can see it on his face, and poor Bob and Bert, our team, are suffering as bad as the rest of our family.

Food supplies are running thin, even

though we've tried hard to stretch them. We still walk all day – what else can we do? – but it looks like we aren't even going anywhere, just seeing the same dirt and rocks over and over. I only hope we soon get to someplace where we can find a home.

September 10 –

I think I can't bear it, it's so hot and dry. No one wants to eat anything at meals, just drink water. Maybe we'll save a bit on food that way, but we've got to eat something to keep up our strength, although some folks say they're about ready to lay down on the trail and die. I get to feeling that way myself at times.

There's no sense in writing in this diary anymore, as there's never anything different, – the same old dry, hot walking all day, every day. I'd been wishing we could travel in the river, instead of alongside, but we veered off away from it to get to the next fort, Fort Boise, so we are even drier now. It seems there is no end to this. Will we ever get there at all, or will somebody just find our poor bones in the desert?

September 17 –

A couple of days ago, we climbed up another of the endless hills, then looked down into

Mona Exinger

this valley with a big green stretch of trees alongside a winding river. Such a welcome sight! This is Fort Boise, which is some foreign word for trees, so even foreign people have the same frank way of naming places we do.

All along the trail, Marcus and I had talked about where to make our home. I kept asking how we'd find a good place for ourselves, and he said it would just have the right look to both of us, and we'd know. Well, we took one look at this lovely green spot by the river, then at each other, and knew this was it, even though we're not at the end of the trail yet.

The train camped for a day at the fort, so Marcus and I each had another chance to think about it while doing our chores. We hurried through a quick supper, then took the children and walked out along the river to look around some more and try to make sure we were thinking straight on this.

It's only a trader's fort with no Army, but still a good thing to have close by, for supplies. And it would be a safe place to go to, in case the Indians out here aren't as nice as the ones we met – what with all the arguing about whose land is whose. This is a likely place for a settlement along the river – which is also called Boise, like the fort – with all those wonderful, cool green trees. It's different from the old home place in Michigan,

Home on the Trail

but that's what we came all this way for, so we thought we'd better give it a try.

I asked the children how they'd feel about not going any farther to Oregon City at the end of the trail, but making a home right here. Hester said she didn't know what Oregon City looked like anyway, and this place seemed nice. Matt was so glad at the thought of not walking any more every day, he just starting running around and whooping it up as his way of saying yes.

We had to go back to camp and tell Cyrus we wouldn't be leaving with the train in the morning. How strange that would seem! Then the part I didn't want to face, but knew I had to – telling our friends goodbye. All the women got together and were so excited to think I'd have a home soon. It was mighty generous of them to be that glad for me, since they had a lot more hard traveling before they could do the same.

I hadn't thought of it since we'd come to Fort Boise, but before getting to Oregon City is another bad stretch of mountains. Then you have the hard choice of going on a road over even more mountains and dry areas, or taking your chances on a raft for a long way down a river. That wasn't what helped us decide, but I was glad we wouldn't have to go through all that.

Mona Exinger

Well, I was brave enough for a while, smiling and talking, then it got to be too much, and I fell into Susannah's arms and cried. She's been such a good friend to me, I couldn't bear to think about staying here and watching her leave, never to be neighbors and not even knowing when we'd meet again. It was like when we left folks in Michigan. I'd already lost Mary Ann, and I didn't want to lose Susannah, too. These folks were all strangers once, but now they're like family, with all we've been through together – the traveling and happiness and heartaches we've shared.

Wouldn't you know it, my crying started off the rest of the women as fast as dry leaves before a wind. Soon enough, it was tears and hankies like nobody's business. We had a good cry all around, and after so many hard times, I think we needed it. Everyone felt better afterward.

Clara came out and said I was a fool for stopping here, but I laughed and said maybe so and hugged her just the same. I believe when she gets all the way to the end of the trail, she'll either find a good home or her comeuppance. God will provide, don't you know? Mrs. Wickham and I shared a wink on that one, and I told Lacey to watch out for married life.

I was so busy with the women I didn't

Home on the Trail

have a chance to notice, but Hester and Matt had gone around and said goodbye to their friends, and Marcus was doing his handshaking with the men. Lots of good-luck wishes, advice, and promises to write were given on both sides. There isn't what you'd call regular mail out here – just relying on folks passing through or maybe the Army or traders going from fort to fort. But we'll hope for the best, and everybody'll have their hands full for quite a while getting settled, anyway.

Marcus and I stayed up that night talking in our wagon about looking for a good home place first, then getting ready for winter. It isn't far off, since we've been traveling so long. Winters are harder here than if we'd gone farther on, but since we're already in our settling place, we have that much more time to get ready. So many things to think about and do! After we'd talked a while, Marcus would snooze off in between my jabbering at him, until I finally couldn't get any answers back. So I lay down myself, and even though I thought I wasn't tired, I was asleep in no time.

The next day we got up and had breakfast the same as usual, but it didn't really feel the same, as we knew we wouldn't be leaving. It was exciting, but hard to watch everybody pack up to go. There were hugs and hand-

Mona Exinger

shakes all around again, and then the train started moving out.

Our family stood together, proud to still be all in one piece and at our new home. We waved as those people we knew so well – most of them real good folks, too – walked away from us to find their own homes farther on. It seemed they left awfully fast, and there we were standing alone outside the fort, watching the dust rise and the wagons disappear into it. We listened to that same old sound of wheels turning and turning, and feet walking and walking.

I felt like crying again, but the children hugged me out of it, so I just laughed at them and me and Marcus and maybe the joy of facing a fresh beginning. We had too much work to do in making ourselves a new life out here to be wasting any time, so we squared our shoulders ready to do it.

September 29 –

My, how busy we've been lately, and how the time has flown! There are so many things to do and not enough hours in the day.

After the wagon train left that morning, Marcus spent the rest of the day looking around for a likely spot for our farm. The children and I took a walk down by the river, try-

Home on the Trail

ing not to feel too lonely. We were trying to get the sound of those wagon wheels out of our heads – even though they were long gone, somehow we could still hear them. Later, I sorted out from the wagon the things we'd need first when Marcus found us a home place. It was odd not to be walking all day.

Marcus came back at supper time, tired and dusty. He said he'd been all over the valley and had decided on a place not too far from the river and the fort. Being the careful type about these things, he'd paced it off and put stakes near the corners of what he was claiming as ours.

We all ate supper, then walked out to take a look. It was a fine place, mostly flat, but sloping down to the river a little, with a nice rise just the right spot for a cabin.

The next day, Marcus started digging a well, since we can't haul water from the river forever, but he gave it over to me as soon as I'd nagged him enough. I told him here I was, an able-bodied soul, with nothing to do but twiddle my thumbs. I wasn't about to do that.

It was hard work, but the children helped by pulling up the buckets of dirt I tied on the end of a rope, while I stayed in the hole getting filthy and, hopefully, closer to water. Hester was a good worker and not any more cross with Matt than she could help, as he

Mona Exinger

got in the way some, trying to do his share.

Our helping freed up Marcus for cutting and hauling logs for our cabin. Mr. McKay, the Hudson's Bay Company man in charge of the fort, says the days'll be warm for a while yet, but the nights get cold, and we'll want more than a wagon to stay in before long. A real cabin, after all these months of only the wagon – I can hardly wait!

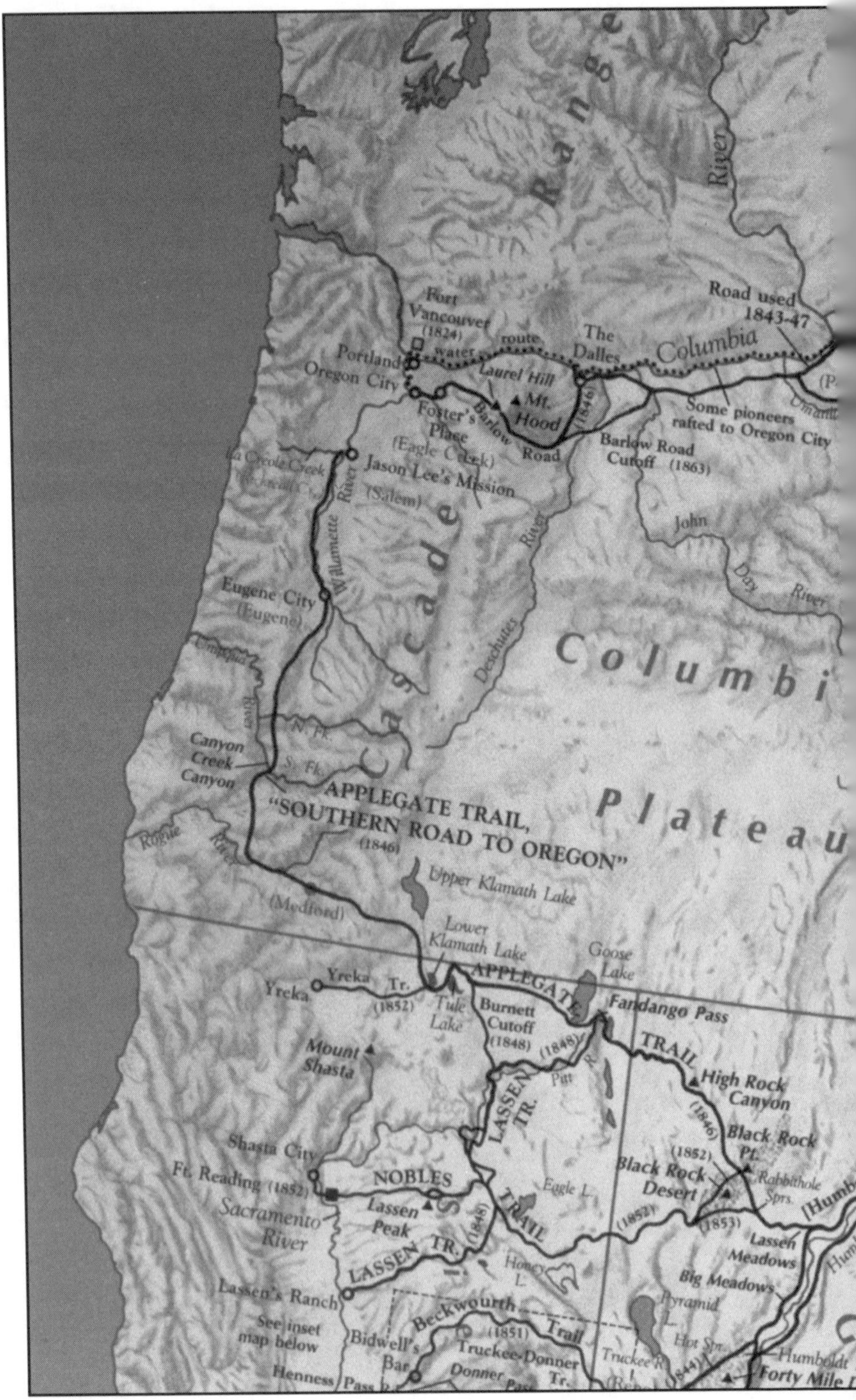
Range
River
Road used
1843-47
Fort
Vancouver
(1824)
water route
Portland
Oregon City
The
Dalles
Columbia
Laurel Hill
Mt.
Hood
Foster's
Place
(Eagle Creek)
Barlow
Road
(1846)
Some pioneers
rafted to Oregon City
Barlow Road
Cutoff (1863)
Jason Lee's Mission
(Salem)
Willamette River
John
Day
River
Deschutes
River
Cascade
Eugene City
(Eugene)
Columbia
Umpqua
River
N. Fk.
S. Fk.
Canyon
Creek
Canyon
APPLEGATE TRAIL,
"SOUTHERN ROAD TO OREGON"
(1846)
Plateau
Rogue
River
Upper Klamath Lake
(Medford)
Lower
Klamath Lake
Goose
Lake
Yreka
Yreka
Tr.
(1852)
Tule
Lake
APPLEGATE
Burnett
Cutoff
(1848)
Fandango Pass
TRAIL
Mount
Shasta
(1848)
Pitt R.
LASSEN TR.
High Rock
Canyon
(1846)
Black Rock
Pt.
(1852)
Black Rock
Desert
Rabbithole
Sprs.
Shasta City
Ft. Reading (1852)
NOBLES
Lassen
Peak
Sacramento
River
(1848)
Eagle L.
TRAIL
(1852)
(1853)
Lassen
Meadows
LASSEN TR.
Honey
L.
Big Meadows
Lassen's Ranch
Pyramid
L.
Beckwourth
(1851)
Trail
See inset
map below
Bidwell's
Bar
Truckee-Donner
Tr.
Donner Pass
Truckee R.
Hot Spr.
Humboldt
Henness Pass
Forty Mile D

Chapter Ten

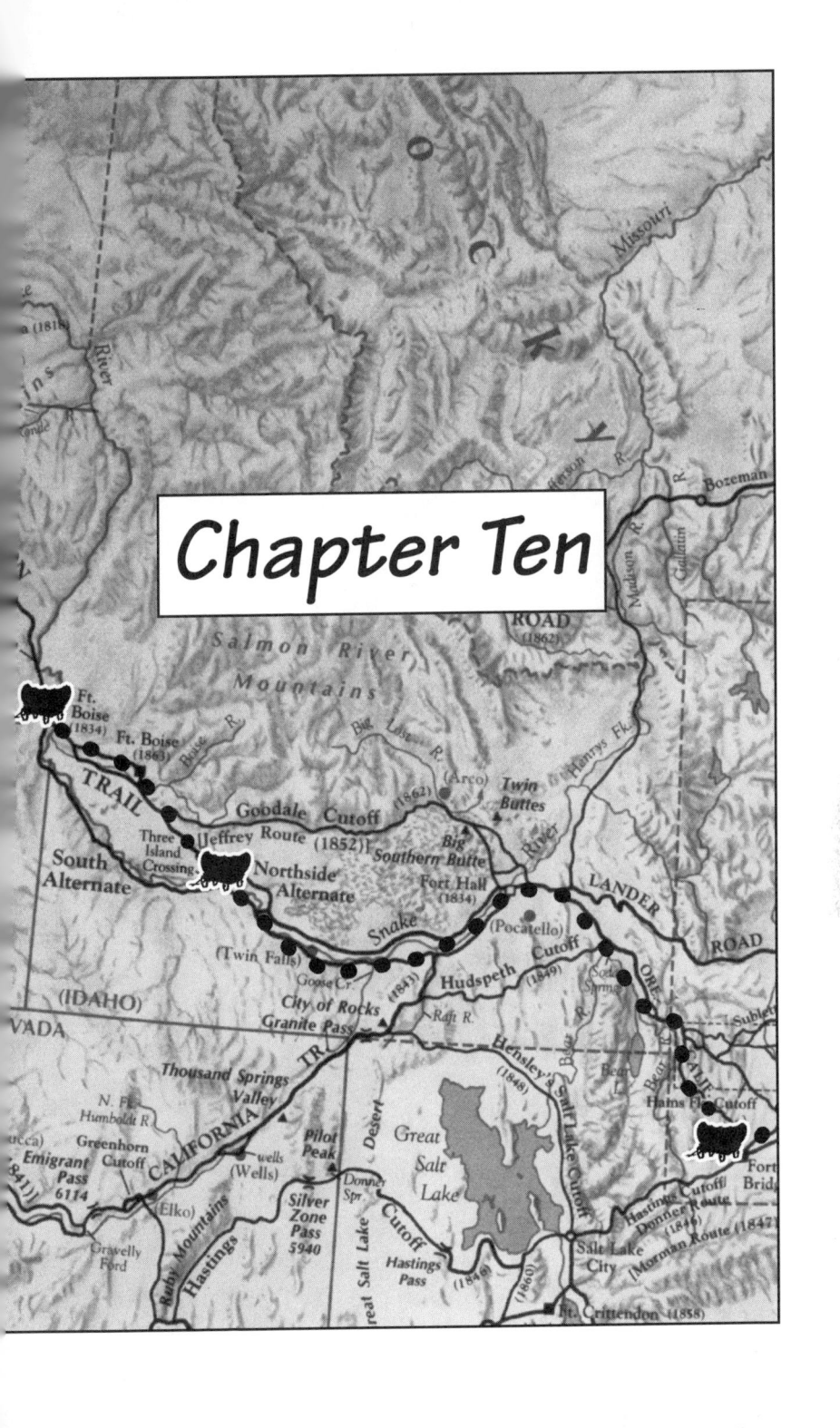

October

October 14 –

You'd think it was the Fourth of July all over again the day I hit water in the well. I let out a whoop, and the children ran and peeked in the hole. They were careful not to get too close, as I'd warned them, but itching to see what was the matter. I hollered it was water, my shoes were soaked, it was almost up to my ankles already, and wasn't it a grand day? Matt lit out like a streak to get Marcus, who was along the river cutting trees. Hester and I sang for joy like bluebirds until the menfolk hove into sight.

When Marcus came back, he grinned down at me, pleased as punch, and said what

Home on the Trail

was the news? I called up proudly it was good clean water to the taste, and how I knew was I'd had ample time to taste it while he was moseying along his slow way back, and by the way, did he think he could spare a moment to haul me up?

Once he dragged me up out of the well – it was a real well now, not just a hole in the ground – Hester took charge of her muddy ma and hustled me off to the wagon to get wet shoes and clothes off me and hot coffee in me. She's a comfort, my Hester.

But all this was some days ago, and we've moved on to other work since. Marcus has gotten quite a pile of logs together for the cabin, but isn't satisfied that it's enough yet. He gets up early in the morning and goes out with his rifle to see if he can flush out a rabbit from the sagebrush or ducks near the river. Several times he's gotten something, and let me tell you, fresh meat tastes mighty good for a change, after all the salt pork we've eaten.

The children are gathering stones for the chimney; that's hard work too, but gives them a chance to play along the river, where a lot of the stones are. I keep busy with Marcus' small hatchet cutting the limbs off the trees in the pile he's made.

We've gotten to know Mr. McKay from the fort a little better, and he comes over to visit from time to time. I thought he was a mighty serious sort at first, but I do believe he's just lonely from being out here where there's not many folks to talk to. He's been kind enough to us and helpful with advice on what the land's like. He and Marcus talk quite a bit about what might be grown here, as it's rather dry.

It seems Marcus is setting his sights on working up a herd of cattle, instead of having the same kind of farm we had in Michigan. He and Mr. McKay think there'd be a call for fresh and dried meat with the folks passing through the fort, and I said maybe they're right, if the charge wasn't too high, like at some of the other forts on the trail.

October 25 –

Tomorrow's wash day, and that's always busy, so I'd best get caught up on my writing today. Just finished a whole passel of letters to the family back East (had to share all the news with Mary Ann) and to many of the friends we met along the trail (a long chatty one to Susannah, I miss her so; one to Mrs. Wickham, to see how she's getting along and if Nathan and Lacey are married yet; and one of thanks to Cyrus for being such a good leader).

I spoke to Mr. McKay about sending letters,

and he was of the opinion I should write to folks at Oregon City, since they'll probably stay close there, wintering over before they fan out to look for their own land in the spring.

There was a train along about ten days after ours – we only visited with them up at the fort for a bit, since we were so busy. Mr. McKay said people are so foolish there might be a few more stragglers left, who started late and are still stumbling along the trail when they should be safe and sound in Oregon City by now. Travelers also come from Oregon City, too – Hudson's Bay men with supplies to stock the fort. They bring dried salmon – fish the Indians sell them – and other things that come all the way around in the ocean from the east. If any more supply men come soon, maybe our letters could go back with them.

I can say honestly all this writing has been a labor for me – my hands are still covered with blisters from cutting limbs off logs. But I did a good job of it, so Marcus said, and he's coming along fine with the cabin. I still help him when there's something I can do without being in the way.

After Hester and Matt gathered heaps of stones for the chimney and hearth, they were glad to turn to something else, even if it was

Mona Exinger

what poor learning I can give them on their reading and sums. I thought it was about time for school to start – though with just us, it's hardly a real school. We work some each morning on it, before beginning our other chores for the day.

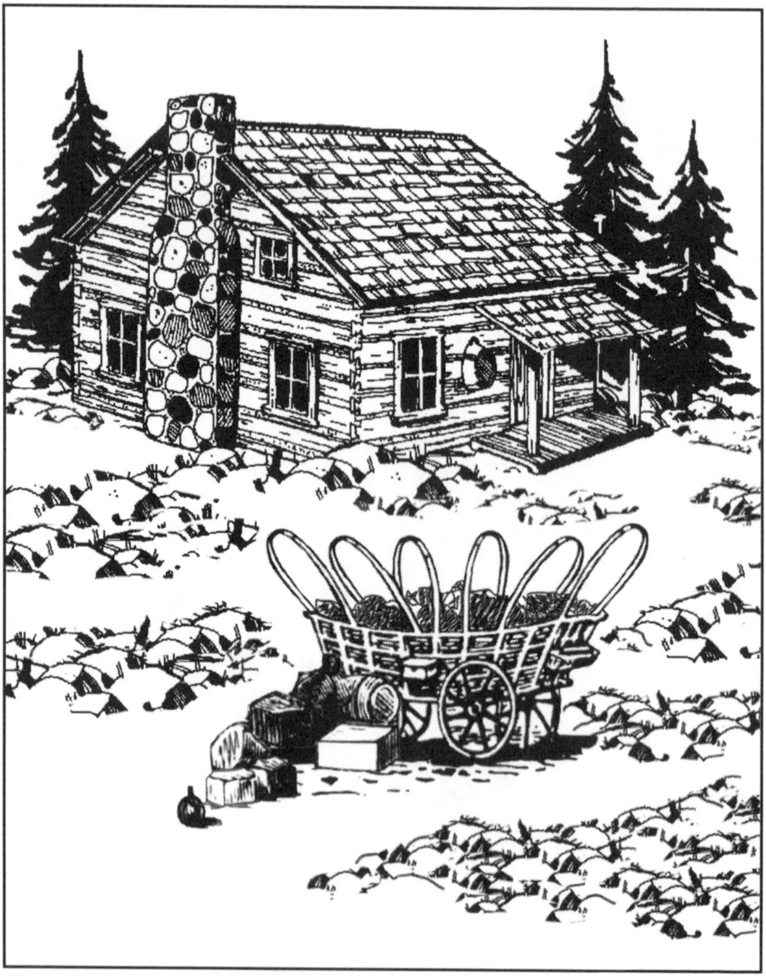

Chapter Eleven

November

November 4 –

Marcus got a deer one frosty morning this week, and we ate well for a few days. I salted the rest away – we're sure to need it later.

He's got the cabin nearly finished, and what a pleasure it is to see the walls of our new home rising! It's been a real family effort, with all of us helping to do what we can. That'll make it that much cozier to live in.

I started doing laundry for Mr. McKay in exchange for some calico for curtains and a few other little things for the cabin. His clothes are in terrible shape – men with no womenfolk often look pretty shabby – so I might offer to do some mending, too.

Home on the Trail

Mr. Goudge, the fort blacksmith, seemed agreeable to my doing his laundry for pay. It'll be a lot of extra work for me, but Hester can help, and the hard cash will be welcome when Marcus sees about getting a few cattle to start our herd next spring.

Laundering for Mr. McKay this winter would help keep our credit at the fort store from getting thick, too. He's been generous in letting us have flour and meal and such, since we hadn't much left when we stopped.

I might say all my washing gives these men a chance to look better for a change, too.

November 16 –

Yesterday was a year exactly since Marcus met Cyrus Bates in our Michigan town so far away and started us on the trail to our new life. I noticed the date in this diary when I was putting things away in the cabin. Thought I'd set this aside for Hester and Matthew when they get older, or even for their children after them. It'll let them know about all the suffering that went into coming out here – and all the joyous times we had, too, and the wondrous things we saw along the way.

When I saw it'd been a whole year – I say a whole year, but it seems much longer, a lifetime practically, for how far we traveled and all we've done – I knew we had to celebrate. So I spun around and saw we didn't have much in the way of party fixings, but I thought we could make do if Matt would catch me a few fish in the river.

Then I hightailed it out to do the inviting, which sounds like a bigger chore than it was. I only had to round up the children, get Hester to sweeping, send Matt off to the river and let Marcus know what I was up to. He was cutting wood for a shed, since Bob and Bert need a new home for the winter, too, and he thought a celebration was a fine idea. He also favored my idea of inviting George – that's Mr. McKay – who's been so good to us here at Fort Boise. So I snatched up my skirts and hauled off to the fort to ask our new friend to celebrate with us.

Well, we hustled around to make our party a fine one. I mixed up my special corncakes, fried them up nice and crisp with Matt's fish, and set the table pretty with some yellow leaves and sumac branches stuck in a jug. We just wore our everyday clothes, but since they don't get full of trail dust anymore, we looked presentable.

George marched up at one o'clock exactly and knocked on our door. When I asked him in, he took his hat off real polite – which was

Home on the Trail

no small doing, since he was carrying two chickens! He said he was a new man with his clothes all clean and ironed and mended these days. It occurred to him a couple of pullets might come in handy for us. He apologized for their being a mite scrawny. But chickens don't come easy around here, and they looked to me like they would fatten up into fine laying hens before too long.

I was so grateful, I could hardly talk straight. Hester took the chickens from George as gentle as could be, and settled them down in the laundry basket. She and Matt started in on plans for making a coop out of tree limbs to keep them in until Marcus gets the shed done, where they can have a corner to themselves.

We sat down to dinner, and everybody ate hearty and talked a lot. George is real friendly when you get to know him. He was glad to have a woman's home-cooked meal for a change, instead of what he and Mr. Goudge and the few other men at the fort can do for themselves – which he says could mostly choke a horse.

He told us some new folks had come in to the fort just the day before, a family called Hastings. They'd been part of the train that came through after ours. They'd had trouble back on the trail when Mrs. Hastings got ill

Mona Exinger

after having a baby. Their train hadn't the patience to wait, as they were already so late in the year, and they left the Hastings family behind to catch up as best they could. That poor family dragged in tired and near starved, so George gave them food to hold them over a bit and advised Mr. Hastings to winter over in the fort. They're not in shape to go any farther, and he thought Marcus and I could help them out and maybe talk them into settling here.

Well, we two shared a look and knew right away we'd do all we could. It's hard enough to travel that far and stay in one piece. But when your train goes off and leaves you with a sick wife and new baby, you need a helping hand, and others ought to find it in themselves to offer it. I said Hester and I would take some fresh bread and call on Mrs. Hastings in the morning to make her comfortable and welcome. Marcus could take Mr. Hastings around to look for a home place and get started cutting some wood before winter.

We chatted on through the afternoon, George talking farming and cattle with Marcus and chicken-keeping with Hester. He told Matt there's two Hastings boys who might like to fish in the river, too, if he cared to show them some good spots. He reeled off for me all the supplies he expected to get with

Home on the Trail

the first big load in the spring. Then he filled in the gaps with whatever gossip and jokes he thought we might find interesting – and with George, we always do.

I put it aside in my mind to tell Mrs. Hastings to send her boys over for what schooling I'm trying to do with the children. That way she'll have some peace and quiet time with the baby while they're out from underfoot. Maybe the boys'll learn something, too. There's always something to do here, just like on the trail, but I didn't come West to be lazy.

The sky was purpling dusk when George got up to leave and thanked us for such a lovely day. We all shook hands with him for bringing the chickens and promised to take the best care of them. He headed off back to the fort, while we stood outside and waved. Then I scooted Hester and Matt in the cabin, as it was chilly, and I don't need sick children on my hands. The door closed behind them on the beginning of a fresh argument about the chicken coop.

Marcus put his arm around me in the cool of the evening, and we stood together, each of us with our own thoughts – that George was a good new friend, and we hoped the Hastingses would be, too; how we'd spent our simple day celebrating the great undertaking of coming out on the trail; what it had meant to leave home and family, make friends and lose some along the way; how we'd struggled to survive and create a new life for ourselves; the work to be done in the days ahead, and how we'd have each other to share it.

We looked around at our land and felt proud. Against the deep purple of the sky, the trees were sharp, black outlines, and the wintering breeze rustled the last of their dry leaves. The river rushed between its grassy banks, a drop of water leaping high, catching the last finger of the day's light to sparkle, and the first evening star winked back at it. This was a fine place, the right place for us, and we knew someday other folks would come, like we had, to help us build one small fort and some scrubby sagebrush into a prospering town – with schools, churches, stores, families, farms, hard work, and laughter.

Even if we didn't go all the way to Oregon City, we knew we'd found ourselves a good new home at the end of our trail.

THE END

Home on the Trail   Mona Exinger

About the author:

Mona Exinger grew up in Michigan, then took a roundabout version of the Oregon Trail herself, stopping to perch briefly in both Oregon and Louisiana before settling in Boise, Idaho. She lives in a circa-1900 house with her husband and three dogs, and believes there's no greater adventure than being on the road, exploring new places. This is her first novel.